PRAISE FOR THE JAMIE JOHNSON SERIES

"You'll read this and want to get out there and play"
Steven Gerrard

"True to the game . . . Dan knows his football"
Owen Hargreaves

"An inspiring read for all football fans"
Gary Lineker

"If you like football, this book's for you"
Frank Lampard

"Jamie could go all the way"
Jermain Defoe

"Pure class – brings the game to life"
Owen Coyle

"I love reading about football and
it doesn't get much better than this"
Joe Hart

"Pure joy"
The Times

"Inspiring"
Observer

"Gripping"
Sunday Express

"A resounding victory"
Telegraph

ABOUT THE AUTHOR

Dan Freedman grew up wanting to be a professional footballer. That didn't happen. But he went on to become a top football journalist, personally interviewing the likes of Cristiano Ronaldo, Lionel Messi, David Beckham and Sir Alex Ferguson. He uses his passion and knowledge of football to write the hugely popular series of Jamie Johnson football novels. When he is not writing, Dan delivers talks and workshops for schools. And he still plays football whenever he can.

www.danfreedman.co.uk
www.jamiejohnson.info
Follow Dan on Twitter @DanFreedman99

DAN FREEDMAN

SCHOLASTIC

First published in the UK in 2009 by Scholastic Children's Books
An imprint of Scholastic Ltd
Euston House, 24 Eversholt Street
London, NW1 1DB, UK
Registered office: Westfield Road, Southam, Warwickshire, CV47 0RA
SCHOLASTIC and associated logos are trademarks and/or registered
trademarks of Scholastic Inc.

This edition published by Scholastic Ltd, 2012

ISBN 978 1407 11605 1

A CIP catalogue record for this book is available from the British Library.

Printed and bound by CPI Group (UK) Ltd, Croydon, CR0 4YY
Papers used by Scholastic Children's Books are made from wood grown in
sustainable forests.

9 10 8

www.scholastic.co.uk/zone

Acknowledgements

Thanks to:

My family – a great team to have behind me.

Joanne – for being such a beautiful muse.

Caspian Dennis, Ena McNamara, Lola Cashman and Sir Trevor Brooking – for your wise advice.

Martin Hitchcock – for telling me I could write.

Frank Lampard and Jermain Defoe – for your support.

Jason Cox – for your fantastic illustrations.

Major – you see things that I don't.

Hazel Ruscoe – this story is inspired by the ideas we had together.

Jo Budd, Anne Romilly, Alex Stone, Ralph Newbrook, Jim Sells and Joe Lyons – for everything you have done to help Jamie Johnson on his way.

And to Sarah Stewart and all the other talented and hard-working people at Scholastic – you have made this all possible…

Play On...

A young boy sits on his grandfather's couch. He has grazes, cuts and wounds all over his legs from where the other boys have fouled him. It was the only way they had been able to stop him...

He squeezes his eyes tight shut as his grandfather puts plasters over his injuries. It hurts...

The grandfather scuffs up the boy's hair with the palm of his hand and smiles...

"If they foul you, JJ, it means they're scared of you. Just keep coming back for more..."

Part One
Eight years later

1

Time to Shine

Thursday 28 May – The day of the Youth Cup Final

Jamie Johnson picked up his gleaming new football boot and kissed it for good luck. Then he slipped his left foot into it.

There were just ten minutes to go until the kick-off of the Youth Cup Final and Foxborough's Academy Director, Steve Brooker, had his young team gathered around him in the dressing room.

"OK, lads, I'm going to keep this brief," he said, looking each one of the players in the eye as he talked.

"You know why we've brought you to this club. We believe that you have something about you – as a footballer and a person – that marks you out as different … that marks you out as a Foxborough player.

"Now the question is: can you bring those attributes, that talent, to the table when it matters most? It's all very well turning it on in training or beating a team in a friendly. But can you do it in a game like tonight – with a full stadium, live on TV, with a proper trophy at stake?

"The truth is that probably only one or two of you will make it into the Foxborough First Team. That's just the way football is. But don't forget, all the other clubs will be watching tonight. This is the biggest advertisement your talent will ever have…

"And I'm not going to lie to you either. We all know that Foxborough is a rich club. The manager can go out any time he wants and buy a fully-paid-up superstar. So why would he pick *any* of you to go into his first team?

"Why? I'll tell you why: because you are all special footballers."

Steve was pacing back and forth along the dressing-room floor in front of his players. Then he turned and stood perfectly still, his eyes shining with intent.

"There are three types of people in life," he said. "There are those who, for whatever reason, do not or cannot recognize an opportunity when it arises. There are those who *do* recognize an opportunity but find themselves unable to take it. And then there are those who see the opportunity and seize it with both hands.

"Tonight, it's time for you to go and show the world who you are and everything we have been working on... Now go and win that trophy!"

As the two teams walked out on to the pristine Foxborough pitch, the bright beam of the floodlights focused their glare on Jamie Johnson – at fifteen the youngest player on either side. He felt a sudden chill of fear shiver up his spine towards his skull.

There were lots of good reasons for him to be nervous tonight. This was the first live TV match that he had ever played in. It was also the first game he had ever played at The Lair, Foxborough's home ground, the biggest stadium in the country. And the referee had his whistle in his mouth and was about to get this crucial game under way any second now...

But the real reason Jamie's body had become stiff with tension was that the big electronic screens inside the stadium had just shown that the entire Foxborough First Team squad, including their captain, Dave Lewington, were all in the ground tonight. They had received a huge cheer from the crowd when they had come up on the screen.

And, as if the players being there wasn't enough, Brian Robertson, manager of Foxborough and one of the most successful managers in the history of football, was also in the crowd.

Tonight, he would be watching Jamie Johnson ... and judging him.

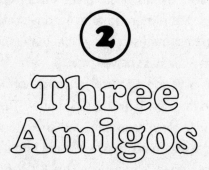

Three Amigos

Seeing Brian Robertson up in the stands had released a curse of nerves in Jamie's body.

He held his hand out in front of him. It was quivering like a crossbar rocked by a thunderbolt of a shot.

He tried to calm himself down. It was still just a football match. All the same rules applied: eleven players against eleven players; whoever scored more goals would win the game. Simple. He just had to get the ball and do his stuff.

But it was no good. Deep down, his stomach had a direct line through his body to his brain and it was saying something else. This wasn't just like any other game. It was the start of his Foxborough career. And he was being watched by Brian Robertson…

As the two teams lined up to shake each other's hands, Jamie took his usual place in between his two room-mates. Xabi Negredo and Antony Asamoah were Jamie's two best mates in the whole team and the three of them were the best players too.

Xabi was a young Spanish left back who tackled so hard they had given him the nickname "The Butcher". Meanwhile, Antony Asamoah, the striker from Ghana, was as fast as lightning. So they called him Bolt.

Standing side by side with The Butcher and Bolt, Jamie could feel his heart start to rise with hope.

They were the *Three Amigos*. All completely different. All great mates. And all fantastic footballers. Between them, they had all the talent required to destroy any team.

Now they just had to go and prove it.

Youth Cup Final
Kick-Off
Foxborough v Harrington

Almost immediately, Foxborough's game plan evaporated in front of them. Steve Brooker had specifically ordered his team not to give away any set pieces in the first fifteen minutes. So Jamie couldn't believe it when they conceded a corner with only three minutes on the clock.

Panic began to spread throughout the Foxborough defence; no one knew who to mark or who was supposed to attack the ball... Then, when the corner came in, Robbie Walters, the Foxborough centre back and captain, made such a wild slash at his attempted clearance that the ball ended up spinning off the outside of his boot and spiralling into the roof of his own net.

It was a horrific own goal. Foxborough were already a goal down.

The worst possible start for Jamie and his teammates.

Youth Cup Final
Foxborough 0 - 1 Harrington
R Walters 06.4

Steve Brooker immediately came out from his dugout to the edge of the technical area to try and urge a response from his team but, for some reason, on this, their big night, they just couldn't find their rhythm.

Yes, they had Bolt, who was six foot two and as fast as anything upfront. And yes, they had Jamie Johnson, the most skilful player on the pitch, out on the wing. But if Foxborough couldn't get them the ball, what use were they?

Jamie only had one chance to go on a run during the

whole of the first half. And he went around his marker so easily that he knew he could take him any time he wanted. But no one was passing him the ball to give him the opportunity to do it again.

It was only Robbie Walters – making amends for his earlier own goal with a looping header just before half-time – that had got Foxborough back on level terms. And they were lucky to be there.

Youth Cup Final
Foxborough 1 - 1 Harrington
R Walters, 41   R Walters OG, 4

As the Foxborough players trudged back to the dressing room, each one of them knew that they had let themselves down. And, if they didn't, Steve Brooker was just about to remind them.

Give it to Jamie

Youth Cup Final
Half-Time
Foxborough 1 - 1 Harrington
R Walters. 41   R Walters OG. 4

"What you lot need to do is forget about the TV cameras," said an angry Steve Brooker, while his players sat looking at the floor.

"And Brian Robertson being here. All that stuff's irrelevant. Remember what I always tell you: this is a simple game – get the ball, pass it to your mate and have a shot on goal… Boys, you have to trust yourselves to play."

Steve's eyes were ablaze with ambition; this was *his* big night as well as his players'.

"And Jamie," he said, turning to face his left-winger. "Their full-back is scared of you. Petrified. You only have to wiggle your hips and he falls over. Trust me. He wants to go home and cuddle his mum! He's had enough!"

The boys laughed but, as their chuckles subsided, Steve was still focusing his attention on Jamie.

"So when you're one-on-one with him, take him on. Every time," he said, pacing steadily towards Jamie. "Show him how good you are. Show everyone how good you are – including yourself."

He put his hand on Jamie's shoulder and gave the muscle above his collarbone a firm but friendly pinch.

"And why don't you try the snake?"

The snake was the new skill that Jamie had been working on for the last few weeks in training.

It was a Brazilian skill in which the attacker flicked the ball outside and then inside of the defender in one rapid movement. If it was done properly, the defender stood no chance; his body and brain would be twisted in different directions before he eventually lost balance. The snake was the single most impossible skill to defend against.

And only Jamie Johnson had the skill, speed and confidence to pull it off.

"Just show it to him once... You'll destroy him."
Steve Brooker smiled. "And lads – let me make this very simple for you: when we get the ball, we give it to Jamie."

Free-Kick Special

Youth Cup Final
Second Half
Foxborough 1 - 1 Harrington
R Walters, 41   R Walters OG, 4

There were fifty-five minutes on the clock when Xabi Negredo curled the ball up the line to Jamie, who had it under control in an instant. This was what he'd been waiting for.

He immediately jinked towards the full-back. Then he shaped to cut inside. The defender lunged off in the direction that he thought Jamie was going, only to find that Jamie hadn't moved at all.

Jamie was still standing in the same position, with his foot resting confidently, almost arrogantly, on top of the ball. Then he did the simplest trick in the football book: he just knocked the ball down the line and chased it.

Simple it may have been, but combined with Jamie's pace, it was also hugely effective.

The two players raced after the ball in a one-on-one test of speed. The defender was giving his all to stay with Jamie but, like so many others, his best was not enough.

Jamie won the race and prodded the ball forward. However, the defender had already committed himself to the tackle, bringing Jamie down right on the very edge of the area. It was a clear free-kick.

Jamie hauled himself up and, while the Harrington goalkeeper frantically organized his wall, the Three Amigos clustered around the ball to discuss their options.

"I'll smash one," suggested Antony.

"I reckon I can bend one into the far corner," said Jamie, eyeing a gap to the keeper's left.

Then an ear-piercing whistle broke up the discussion.

It was Steve Brooker. He was holding up two fingers on one hand and, behind them, one finger from another.

The boys knew who he wanted to take it: Xabi. They were going to use a free-kick routine they had been working on in training. Jamie and Antony were to stand directly in front of the ball, with their backs to the Harrington wall. They were providing a protective screen so that neither the players in the wall nor the goalkeeper could see how the ball was going to be struck or, crucially, when. The element of surprise was the key.

Antony and Jamie took up their positions, puffing their chests out and standing as tall as they could to completely shield the ball from view. Then, a second before Xabi was about to strike the ball, they peeled away in opposite directions, to leave the route to the goal clear.

The Butcher's strike was crisp, precise and brimming with power.

Jamie knew it was in as soon as Xabi hit it. He'd seen it enough times in training. Xabi was a free-kick specialist; he always found the target and when this boy hit a ball, it stayed hit.

The ball arced and swung over the wall. It homed in on its target with laser-like accuracy. It swerved, dipped and fizzed, all the while staying on course for the top left-hand corner of the goal. It seemed to be getting even faster as it whooshed into the net.

It was there! A Xabi Negredo special!

By the time his teammates looked around, Xabi was already on his knees, sliding across the turf towards the corner flag. That was something he'd practised in training too!

"*Gol! Gol! Gol!*" Xabi was shouting to himself, punching his fist against his chest. He was so happy he was almost crying. He crossed himself and kissed his fingers with a flourish. Then he looked to the sky with a dramatic expression on his face.

It was such a professional celebration that Jamie and Antony felt almost rude to interrupt it by piling on top of him. But they did anyway, kissing Xabi's cheek for good measure!

⑤
Jamie's Move

Youth Cup Final
Foxborough 2 - 1 Harrington
R Walters. 41   R Walters 06. 4
X Negredo. 59

Now Foxborough were beginning to motor. The millions of miles that their scouts had travelled in order to assemble this team of starlets was beginning to pay off.

Steve Brooker's careful approach had brought them together as a powerful team. And now Jamie Johnson, the jewel in the crown, was ready to announce his talent to the watching public.

Sprinting back towards his own goal, Jamie quickly

caught up with a Harrington midfielder, who was bringing the ball out of his own half. As the Harrington player searched for someone to pass to, he was becoming hesitant … vulnerable.

Jamie slid along the grass and hooked his foot cleanly around the ball. Then he sprang back up on to his feet, flicking the ball forward in the same movement.

Jamie flew into Harrington territory at his very top speed. He was a leopard, chasing down his prey – the Harrington full-back.

The defender was standing on the edge of his area, waiting. He had been left alone – exposed and unprotected by his teammates. He was defenceless.

It was almost possible to detect a glint of a smile on Jamie's face as he powered towards his cowering opponent.

Jamie was completely in control. Of the ball. Of his body. Of the situation…

He nudged the ball forward – slowly, softly, almost teasing the defender's brain with the possibility of making a challenge. But the defender wouldn't bite, he wouldn't go for it; he just kept backing away further and further towards his own goal.

Jamie knew that, to get past him, he was going to have to beat him.

Fine, Jamie thought to himself. *If that's the way you*

want it, that's the way you can have it. And with that, Jamie unleashed his skills.

His left foot swept the ball outwards and then back inside so swiftly that the defender would've had to watch the move in ultra slow motion to even be able to work out where the ball was, never mind intercept it!

It wasn't until Jamie was long gone that the Harrington full-back realized that Jamie had beaten him on the inside with – what else? The snake.

Now Jamie bore down on the goal. He was just ten yards out.

The keeper scurried off his line to shut down the angles. He hunched down and put his gloved hands up as though Jamie were threatening him with a weapon.

Jamie pulled his left foot as far back as he could. It seemed clear he was going to blast the ball into the back of the net.

The keeper steadied himself, ready for a missile of a shot.

So he was shocked when Jamie slipped his left foot under the ball and, with simple grace, craftily chipped it high above him.

The goalkeeper raised his hands into the air and arched his body backwards, but both he and Jamie knew there was no point. He was never going to save that ball. It had been chipped too perfectly for the goalkeeper to get anywhere near it.

The ball bounced once and, even before it had hit the net, Jamie already had his arms outstretched, awaiting the rush of his teammates to celebrate the strike.

As they engulfed him, Jamie stood tall and, with a broad smile, pointed a finger of gratitude back towards the applauding Steve Brooker in the dugout.

It was an individual goal. It combined pace, skill and football intelligence.

It had Jamie Johnson written all over it.

Youth Cup Final
Foxborough 3 - 1 Harrington

R Walters. 41	R Walters 06. 4
X Negredo. 59	
J Johnson. 68	

6

A Striker's Hunger

As they jogged back to the centre circle, Jamie heard the stadium announcer call out his name. The Foxborough crowd gave a big cheer. Jamie kissed his clenched fist and raised it up to the sky.

"Oi!" shouted Steve Brooker from the touchline.

His players were still giving each other high fives as Harrington were about to restart the game. Steve Brooker was fuming. How many times had he told them that you are at your most vulnerable just after you've scored? There is always pride before the fall.

"This game's not over yet!" he yelled, hurling his bottle of water down to the ground.

His boys turned and nodded. They understood that it wasn't the Foxborough way to ever let up. They had to keep going until the very end. And there were more goals for them in this match – if they wanted them.

For the next ten minutes, Foxborough played keep ball. Their possession was suffocating any Harrington hopes of a comeback. Soon, the Harrington players started to chase with less vigour. Their movements became slower as they gradually gave in to Foxborough's stranglehold on the game.

The Foxborough fans began to openly celebrate their team's superiority. The shouts of *"Olé!"* went up as the Foxborough defenders taunted the Harrington strikers by passing the ball along the width of their back line.

But this was all too easy for Jamie. Boring, even.

He cantered in from the wing to the centre of the pitch and practically tackled his own central midfielder to take possession of the ball. Then he began to dribble with it.

In and out of the tackles he glided, powering past players, hurdling over legs, springing through gaps and dodging beyond desperate lunges. His talent was there for all to see.

He had the whole crowd on their feet. They knew they were witnessing something special and now Jamie was ready to give them exactly what they wanted. He was going to bend one into the top corner.

He'd set his body and was just swinging his leg around towards the ball when he was violently shoulder-barged to the ground by the Harrington centre-half.

The referee blew his whistle immediately. It was such a clear penalty that even the defender didn't bother to dispute it. His only aim had been to take Jamie down.

Jamie clawed the ball to his chest and sprang back on to his feet like a boxer trying to prove that a punch hadn't hurt him. Scoring the penalty would be the perfect way for him to take his revenge.

Jamie put the ball on the spot and took three steps back. *Still go for the top corner*, he told himself. *Never change your mind when you're about to take a p—*

Then Jamie felt the pain of two fingers jabbing their way into his ribs.

It was Bolt.

"Let me take it, man," he appealed.

"Leave it, Bolt," said Jamie. "I won it. It's my—"

"You've already scored tonight! I haven't. Come on, man; I'm a striker, I need my goal..."

Jamie looked Bolt in the eye. He could see the hunger that made him the player he was. He was so desperate to score. So determined to get his name on the scoresheet.

Jamie let him have it.

Although neither Jamie nor Bolt were aware of it, something very unusual was happening as Bolt stepped up to take that penalty: while everyone else in the ground had their eyes on the ball as it scorched into the roof of the net, two people – two very important people – weren't even looking at the action.

They were looking at the winger whose run had just won the penalty.

Way up in the stands, the Foxborough Assistant Manager, Tommy Taylor, had leaned across to his boss, Brian Robertson, and whispered something in his ear. Some sort of question, or suggestion…

Brian Robertson seemed to think for a second, taking in what Tommy Taylor had said. Then, slowly at first, he nodded his head. He had made a judgement.

Youth Cup Final
Final Score
Foxborough 4 - 1 Harrington

R Walters, 41	R Walters OG, 4
X Negredo, 59	
J Johnson, 68	
A Asamoah, 82 (pen)	

Foxborough win the
Youth Cup Final

⑦
Remember the Name

The Foxborough players went up on to the podium and, one by one, they shook hands with a man that Jamie didn't recognize – he assumed it was one of the sponsors – and collected their medals. Then, to a huge cheer, Robbie Walters, the Foxborough captain, lifted the trophy.

Loud music blared around the stadium and fireworks were let off behind the Foxborough players' heads. When Robbie passed the trophy down the line, each one of the Foxborough players kissed it and lifted it into the air.

To Jamie, it seemed that more camera flashbulbs

went off for him than had been the case for the other players. Or perhaps he was just more aware of the flashes when they were focused on him.

As they got down from the podium, the players saw the end of Steve Brooker's TV interview. He was talking to Esther Vaughan. She was a reporter on TV and she also did adverts for hair shampoo. Jamie had a poster of her on his wall.

"Of course I'm proud," Steve was saying to Esther. "But it's not about me, it's about this young team. They all played for each other and they got exactly what they deserved tonight."

"Thanks very much," Esther said to Steve after the interview had finished. "I really appreciate that. If we can just have a few words with Jamie, then that's us done."

Jamie's head twitched. He was sure he had heard right. He was sure they wanted to interview him. Esther Vaughan wanted to interview *him*!

"Sorry, love," said Steve. "No academy players do TV interviews. Orders from the top. Mr Robertson is very strict about young players getting overexposed to the media. Out of my hands, I'm afraid, love."

As Steve Brooker walked away, Esther's features changed. Her soft, attractive smile dissolved into a cold, stern stare.

"He's the man of the match, Steve," she called. "It's part of the contract and you know it. We don't pay all this money to have zero access."

Steve turned around and put his hands on his hips. It was the same position he took up when he was thinking about making a substitution.

"Two minutes," he said. "And nothing clever! Otherwise I'll be the one who gets it in the neck from Mr Robertson."

"Deal," she agreed.

Steve looked around. Jamie quickly knelt down and pretended to be doing up his laces.

"Jamie!" Steve shouted.

Jamie pretended not to hear.

"Jamie!"

"Me?" Jamie asked, innocently.

"The TV people want to do a quick interview with you," said Steve, putting his arm around Jamie. "I know you haven't started your media training yet but I think it'll be good experience for you. You OK with that?"

"Yeah, whatever you say, boss," said Jamie.

"OK, Esther," said Steve, bringing Jamie over to the reporter. "Here he is. Remember, two minutes."

At first Esther Vaughan just ignored Jamie. She was

listening to someone talking in her ear and looking at herself in a small mirror that she held in her hand.

Jamie was looking at her too. She had the most beautiful reddish-brown hair he had probably ever seen. He wondered if there was some unwritten law that said you had to be seriously attractive to work in TV.

Then Esther's face suddenly came alive and she shone her eyes on Jamie.

"Hi there, Jamie," she said, shaking his hand.

Jamie felt embarrassed that his hands were all hot and sweaty. Hers were cool and clean.

"All right," he said, discreetly trying to spike up his hair before the interview. The sweat on his hands could act as a makeshift type of gel.

"I'm just going to ask you a couple of questions about the game," she smiled. "Nothing too tricky."

"That's cool." Jamie laughed. He was feeling more confident now.

"OK," said Esther. "They're coming to us in two..." Then she put one finger up and pointed to the cameraman, who turned on a set of lights. They were so bright they almost blinded Jamie.

"Thanks, Gary. Yes, I'm here with the star of tonight's show, Jamie Johnson."

Jamie tried to raise a smile but suddenly all he could think about was the fact that he was live on TV. Anyone could be watching. People could be laughing at him. Was the camera going in so close on his face that everyone could see his spots? What if he swore? He mustn't sw—

"—what do you think about that, Jamie?"

Jamie hadn't heard a word of what she'd just said!

"Sorry ... could you say that again, please?" he mumbled. He sounded like an idiot!

"Some of the journalists here were saying that that was one of the most promising individual performances they had ever seen from a player in a Youth Cup Final. What do you think about that?"

Jamie's mind had gone completely blank. His mouth was so dry he wasn't sure he'd be able to get any words out even if he did know what to say – which he didn't. Playing against the world's best defender would be easier than this interview.

He tried to calm himself down. He'd seen loads of footballers doing interviews. He could just try and copy the way they usually spoke.

"Well ... obviously it's nice to get praise ... and what have you ... but tonight is not about me, it's about Foxborough ... and the team ... I thought everyone did brilliant."

"Quite. But that was some solo goal you scored. Talk us through that one, Jamie."

"Well, I managed to beat my man and then I had a shot and, luckily enough for me, it went in. I was just happy to see it go in, really."

Esther was still nodding as though she was expecting Jamie to say something else. But he had nothing else *to* say!

"Great ... and what does it mean for you to play for Foxborough now, because a little birdie tells me that you are actually a Hawkstone United fan?"

Jamie went bright red. How did she know? He hadn't even told any of his teammates!

"Well ... kind of ... Mike ... my granddad used to play for them and he took me there when I was really ... like ... young, so I sort of supported them when I was younger and that ... but now I'm Foxborough all the way and I'm really happy to be here. This is definitely the biggest club in the country."

"So there's no truth in rumours linking you with the big European clubs, then? Because you're not old enough to actually sign a professional contract with Foxborough yet, are you? So, when the time comes, theoretically, you could still join any other club."

Suddenly Jamie became aware of Steve Brooker's presence beside him. Steve was staring angrily at Esther, drawing his finger across his throat, demanding that she finish the interview immediately.

"Erm … well, I just play football," Jamie stammered. "I leave all the other stuff to my dad. But I'm really happy here. The only way I'd leave Foxborough is if they didn't want me any more."

"Well, I don't think there's much chance of that!" Esther said, laughing. "OK, back to you, Gary, and I guess it's a case of Jamie Johnson – remember that name!"

Jamie wiped the sweat from his forehead. That had definitely been the toughest part of the whole evening. Now he knew why Foxborough gave their players media training!

"Thanks, Jamie," said Esther, giving him an extra-special smile as the cameraman started packing up all the electrical gear. "Good luck for the rest of the season. See you again sometime."

"I'll look forward to it," said Jamie over his shoulder as he headed back to the dressing room.

Nice line, he congratulated himself. How come he was suddenly able to talk again as soon as the camera wasn't pointed at him?

8

"The Night is Young"

Back in the changing room, Jamie had a quick shower, did his hair and got changed. When he turned on his phone, he had two missed calls and three texts.

The texts were from his mum, his dad and one from Jack. His girlfriend.

.ıll 🔋 📤

✉ Messages

MUM MOB

Watched the whole game! You got it in the net brilliantly. Very proud. Mum x P.S. Mike came over after too. He says you deserved MOM (?)

Options   **Reply**   Menu

Messages

DAD
Nice 1, Jamie — but how come u didn't take the penalty?! Business meeting. Me and u 2morrow. 2 p.m. after training. Don't worry about going 2 school, I'll feed them an excuse. Dad

Options   **Reply**   Menu

Messages

JACK
Just leaving the gym — watched you play while I went on the treadmill. You were amazing — and I ran 6 km! Call me as soon as u can! Can't wait 2 spk 2 U! J xxx

Options   **Reply**   Menu

Jamie selected Jack's number and was just about to press *call* when he received a large slap on his back.

"Come on, TV star, let's go," shouted Bolt. "The night is young."

As the doors at the back of the Foxborough stadium were unlocked to let the players out, the Three Amigos were greeted by a massive cheer. Jamie heard his name being called as a barrage of camera flashes went off.

From his side, a river of youngsters nudged and elbowed their way in front of him.

34

"Can I have your autograph, please, Jamie?" they clamoured, jostling for position, while shoving their notepads under his nose.

Jamie's mind flowed back to when he was at school, dreaming of becoming a professional footballer, practising his signature on the back of his exercise books. His teachers had gone mad when they had caught him. None of them believed he would ever make it as a famous footballer.

"Sure," Jamie said to the autograph hunters. "Have you got a pen?"

"Well done, my friends!" Hassan beamed as the boys got into the car. He was a driver for Foxborough and his job was to take the three boys to and from all training sessions and home matches.

There was no doubt that the boys had got lucky. Not only was Hassan a cool guy – he talked to them about girls all the time – but he also had the best car out of any of the drivers.

"When you are famous, I tell all my friends back home that I know you! That I drive you!" smiled Hassan.

The boys laughed and gave Hassan high fives.

"Now, I take you home?" he asked.

"No home tonight," said Xabi. "Tonight is fiesta!"

"Are you sure?" said Hassan. "Is OK with the boss?"

"Yeah, it's cool," Jamie reassured him. "He said we can go out 'cos we won. Take us into town, please, Hassan!"

"OK," he said. "Here we go!"

Hassan revved his engine and put his foot down.

Once they got into town, it took only a few minutes for Xabi to be surrounded by a group of girls. There must have been ten of them. They all wanted to feel his six-pack.

Xabi and girls seemed to go together like thunder and lightning – one was never far behind the other.

Jamie shook his head. It was a gift. Xabi had it and Jamie didn't.

"Jamie, come here," Xabi smiled, beckoning Jamie over.

Jamie was just about to go over, when his phone rang. It was Jack. He'd already had two missed calls from her earlier that evening, which was strange; she normally just left one missed call and then waited for Jamie to call her back…

"Jamie!" Xabi demanded again. "These girls want to meet you!"

Jamie looked at his phone again. Then he turned it to silent.

9

Paper Talk

Friday 29 May

The next morning, the Three Amigos woke up in the same way as they did every day – to the sound of the radio in the kitchen, as Mrs Luscombe cooked up their breakfast.

Mrs Luscombe had been doing this job for Foxborough – housing and feeding their young players who did not have family in the local area – for the last twenty years.

The Butcher, Bolt and Jamie were Mrs Luscombe's current "tenants" and today she was cooking them an extra-special breakfast to congratulate them on their big win last night.

"Come on, you two!" Jamie said, banging on the bathroom doors. There were two bathrooms but, no matter what time Jamie got out of bed, he somehow always seemed to lose the morning race.

He listened at the doors. The showers were on in both. At least another ten minutes to wait. By now, Jamie knew Bolt and Xabi's morning routine better than they did.

The boys were so close that it was strange to think that, had it not been for Foxborough, they would never have met at all.

Bolt had been recommended to the club by Foxborough's scout in Africa. He'd broken all scoring records in Ghana and, when the scout had sent back a DVD of Bolt in action, Foxborough had snapped him up immediately.

Meanwhile, Steve Brooker, the Foxborough Academy Director, had himself come across Xabi Negredo during a youth tournament in Spain last summer.

Xabi's Spanish club had been very angry and accused Foxborough of poaching their young player – they had even threatened to take the case to court – but in the end the two clubs had come to an "agreement" which allowed Xabi to join Foxborough.

Jamie Johnson, on the other hand, had perhaps had the most unusual route into Foxborough Academy. It had all started with a phone call that Steve Brooker had received. He'd been at his desk at the academy when a call came through from a man called Ian Reacher. How he'd managed to get through to Steve's direct line was still a mystery.

Reacher had gone on to tell Steve about a talent that he could not afford to miss. A boy called Jamie Johnson. A left-winger who was playing in the Interschool Cup Final that afternoon.

"I'm his agent," Reacher had said. "This boy is hot – believe me. I'm telling you, if you don't snap him up, someone else will. It's first come, first served…"

Steve Brooker never normally followed up random calls like this. Nine times out of ten it was either someone playing a prank or else someone who hoped to make a quick buck. But he had heard of this Jamie Johnson from a couple of his regional scouts, so off Steve Brooker had gone, pretty much on a flyer.

It turned out to be one of the best decisions Steve Brooker had ever made. Within twenty minutes of seeing Jamie Johnson kick a football, Steve had offered him a trial at Foxborough. He couldn't believe his luck that Johnson hadn't already been snapped up by another club.

There was only one piece of the Jamie Johnson jigsaw that did not quite seem to fit for Steve Brooker. It turned out that Ian Reacher was this lad Jamie Johnson's dad. Why hadn't he mentioned that in the first place?

"'Rayyyy!" The Butcher and Bolt cheered sarcastically as Jamie came into the breakfast room. They were clapping him and laughing. Jamie had no idea what was going on.

"Here he is!" joked Bolt. "One half of the famous couple! Sold the rights to your wedding yet?!"

Jamie scrunched his eyebrows and looked at his teammates convulsing with laughter as they waved a newspaper around in front of him.

"Guys … what are you going on about?" Jamie asked.

"Show him, Xabi, show him!" shouted Bolt, ripping the newspaper out of Xabi's hands, putting it on the table in front of Jamie.

Jamie looked at the front page. He still had no idea what his two mates were laughing about.

"'Car Crash Kills Four'," Jamie read the headline out loud. "What's so funny about tha—"

"Not there!" said Xabi, flipping the pages of the paper forward. "Here!"

He opened the paper to page four and Jamie got the shock of his life.

There was a huge photo of Jack under the headline:

"Is This Soccer's New Queen Wag?"

Jamie sat down and, trying to ignore Xabi and Bolt's banter, attempted to read the story.

TODAY PAGE

Is This Soccer's New Queen WAG?

● While her boyfriend, Jamie Johnson, was wowing TV viewers in the Youth Cup Final last night, the new WAG on the football scene was still leading a normal life.

Our exclusive photos show fifteen-year-old Jack Marshall arriving home from the gym, where she had no doubt watched her childhood sweetheart lead the Foxborough youngsters to victory with a match-winning performance.

But while Johnson – who ditched his real name of Reacher when his dad left home – is the star attraction on the pitch, Jack is most definitely the stunner off it. She may still live in the same street that she and Johnson grew up in, but Jack Marshall's life could be about to change – in a big way!

With her glamorous long legs and natural beauty, stylists and modelling agencies will be on red alert.

"Jack definitely has the face and figure to go on the catwalk," said one top model spotter.

Lucky Jamie Johnson has it all. So, the question is, are he and Jack Marshall sport's new golden couple?

Red

2005
place
as ne
not to
comn
is usu
issues

Jamie put down the paper. His face had gone bright red. No wonder Jack had been trying to get hold of him so desperately last night. He immediately got out his phone and called her. But it went straight to voicemail – she was probably already at school.

Hopefully, Jamie would be able to see her tonight, though. Steve Brooker had told them that they might get the weekend off, so Jamie was planning to head back home.

"Well?" said Bolt, thrusting an imaginary microphone under Jamie's chin. "Any comment from the superstar?"

"No," said Jamie. "All interview requests must go through my agent!"

10
Driving Ambition

As the three young prodigies waited for Hassan to come and pick them up, Jamie could not have been happier.

He was settled in Foxborough and had just played the game of his life.

It was all a far cry from the first few weeks after he'd left home.

Before Jamie had been placed with Mrs Luscombe, he and his dad had had to share a room in a Travelodge on the outskirts of Foxborough.

At first, Jamie had thought it would be fun and would give him and his dad a chance to get to know each other again, but Jamie's dad seemed to have business meetings every night. That left Jamie by himself in the hotel room.

Even though he was really homesick, he didn't even want to call home in case his new stepdad, Jeremy, answered the phone. It made Jamie feel really weird, imagining another person living at *his* house.

In those first few difficult weeks, the only person who Jamie could actually talk to was Jack. Every night, when his dad went out, Jamie would call her. He didn't know how many free minutes he had on his phone deal. He didn't care. He just knew he had to speak to her.

Stupid things, like hearing what she'd done at school, what her mum had made for dinner – they were things that cheered Jamie up the most. In a different place, away from everything he knew, it was Jack that reminded Jamie of home.

At exactly 10 a.m. Hassan hooted his customary three belts on his horn and the Three Amigos all piled in for the drive to training.

As Hassan approached the security barrier outside the training complex, some of the Foxborough fans pointed and shouted at the car: "Hey! There are the youth team lads! Well played last night, lads! Future Foxborough legends, you lot!"

The Three Amigos laughed and waved back. It

was the first time any of the fans outside the training ground had recognized them. It showed how big last night's game was.

As ever, the First Team players' cars made the training complex look like the forecourt of a luxury car salesroom. All over the place multi-millionaire footballers were arriving in their 4 x 4s, Lamborghinis and Ferraris.

Jamie was looking at the Foxborough captain, Dave Lewington, as he parked his big black Bentley. Jamie thought that the car reflected Dave himself: top of the range, sleek and most definitely classy.

It was life in the fast lane and Jamie wanted to be a part of it.

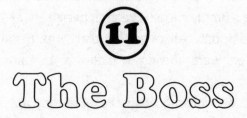

The Boss

"OK, firstly, well done again for last night," said Steve Brooker, clapping his hands together. He seemed in a particularly good mood.

"I've had a personal chat with the boss this morning—"

"Get a pay rise, did you, boss?" teased Bolt, earning a laugh from his teammates.

"Thank you for that, Antony!" smiled Steve. "Anyway, Mr Robertson asked me to pass on his congratulations to you. He says 'well done' and agrees that you all fully deserve your weekend off."

"Yes!" the Foxborough boys collectively responded. If Jamie caught the early train, he could be back home by eight o'clock.

"I'll assume that you'll all be taking the opportunity to catch up on some lost sleep because, and you can correct me if I'm wrong, I believe I can detect a few bags under people's eyes this morning."

Jamie, Bolt and The Butcher looked at each other and grinned. It had been a good night.

"So let's get out there and loosen those muscles out from the match," said Steve.

As the lads piled out on to the training pitch and started kicking balls around in different directions, Steve Brooker pulled Jamie back by his collar.

"Boss wants to see you," he said in a serious voice.

"Me?" said Jamie. "Why?"

"He'll tell you himself."

Jamie closed his eyes. He already knew the reason.

Brian Robertson ruled Foxborough with both an iron fist and a soft touch. Everyone at the club, even the senior players, feared him. But at the same time, he could make you feel the greatest player in the world if he paid you even the slightest compliment. A "not bad" from Brian Robertson meant you'd just played the game of your life!

When he'd said hello to Jamie on his first day in the Foxborough Academy, Jamie had thought he might explode with pride. That's how he could make you feel, with just one word.

But, if you got on his wrong side, he could destroy you. He had a special way of "disciplining" his players. He would come up close to you and shout so hard and so loud that you could feel his hot breath gust like a hurricane into your face. The players called it the hairdryer treatment.

And, if there was one thing that Brian Robertson couldn't stand, it was his players doing too many interviews. He thought it meant that they weren't concentrating enough on their football. "You're either a footballer or you're in show business," he'd once said. "You can't do both."

And the worst crime of all in Robertson's book was a young player getting involved with the press before he'd even made a name for himself in the game.

With him and Jack plastered all over the papers this morning, Jamie knew what was coming. He prepared himself for the hairdryer treatment as he knocked timidly on the door, which had *Manager* emblazoned on the outside.

"Come in," was the reply. Robertson's deep, gruff voice was one of the most famous sounds in football.

Jamie pushed the heavy door open. Robertson was sitting behind his desk. He was on the phone and watching the scrolling headlines of Sports News on the

TV at the same time. He motioned to Jamie to sit on the couch.

Jamie nervously shuffled his way across the room. His back was to Robertson, who was now shouting angrily down the phone.

"What?" he demanded. "They can't suspend him for that! A fool could see that wasn't a deliberate elbow! What do those idiots know about football anyway?! Tell them we'll be appealing!"

And with that, he slammed down the phone so hard, Jamie could feel himself flinch.

Jamie looked around Brian Robertson's office. He imagined Robertson signing world-famous footballers for Foxborough in this room … on this couch!

"Do you know what I want to talk to you about, son?" asked Brian Robertson, as he sat down opposite Jamie. He was wearing training shorts, and Jamie could see a blue vein throbbing in his calf. He'd been a striker when he used to play.

Jamie felt like he was in the head teacher's office about to get the biggest telling off of his life.

"Yes, sir … boss … Mr Robertson… I'm really sorry, it won't happen again…"

Brian Robertson stared at Jamie. As the clock ticked in the corner of the room, Jamie waited for his manager to vent his fury.

And then Brian Robertson smiled.

"Well, you'd better make it happen again, son," he growled. "You were a different class last night. I want you to train with us today."

Behind the Dressing-Room Door

Jamie was still trying to take in everything that was happening when Tommy Taylor, Brian Robertson's assistant, appeared at the doorway.

"Morning, gaffer," he said cheerily. "The lads are all here. Shall I take Jamie over?"

Brian Robertson nodded and picked up his phone again. Jamie could sense it was time for him to leave. On his way out, he knocked over a pile of match DVDs that were resting on the table but he managed to pick them up without Robertson noticing. He hoped.

Jamie took in a deep gulp of air as Tommy Taylor opened the door to the First Team dressing room. Jamie had always wondered what lay behind the door of a Premier League dressing room. And now, as that door opened, a new world revealed itself to Jamie.

The Foxborough stars were all there – every single one of them. They were the league leaders, about to be crowned Premier League Champions for the second season in a row. Every single one of these players was a multi-millionaire. And Jamie was staring at them, open-mouthed, as if they were an exhibit in some kind of football museum.

Putting his arm around Jamie, Tommy Taylor said: "Lads, this is Jamie Johnson, the winger from the Youth Team last night. He's with us today."

Jamie could feel his whole face burn with embarrassment.

Not that any of the players noticed. In fact, none of them had even looked up because, although Tommy Taylor was Robertson's right-hand man, he didn't have the same authority as the manager. As far as anyone could tell, all Tommy Taylor seemed to do was agree with Robertson and repeat what he had just said back to him!

The First Team players barely registered any reaction

52

to Tommy and Jamie's presence. They simply carried on with what they were doing, which was talking on the phone to their agents or their girlfriends.

Jamie couldn't believe the amount of bling there was in one dressing room. There was enough to open up a diamond shop!

"Well played last night, mate," said Dave Lewington, the Foxborough club captain, finally acknowledging Jamie's existence. "Good to have you with us," he smiled, shaking Jamie's hand firmly. "Enjoy it today."

For the warm-up before training, the Foxborough players divided themselves into pairs, leaning on each other as they stretched. Jamie didn't have a partner so he stretched his hamstrings by himself.

He could feel every muscle in his body tighten when he saw Brian Robertson walk out from his office to take his place on the side of the pitch. Then Tommy Taylor got training under way.

First it was set pieces, followed by shooting practice. And then it was time for a game.

Jamie knew that the worst thing that he could do was think. If he thought too much, he'd start to realize that he was a fifteen-year-old training with the Foxborough First Team. And if he realized that, then his game would most likely go to pieces.

Instead, he imagined that he was a South American superstar who had just signed for Foxborough for a world-record transfer fee. That made him feel more confident.

Now he was ready to play.

In the game, Jamie was up against the Foxborough right back, Rick Morgan. Morgan was a tall and athletic player who had made over three hundred appearances for Foxborough. He'd been one of the best right backs in the country for what seemed like decades and everyone at Foxborough called him Wolf.

Jamie had no idea why his nickname was Wolf; the only thing he did know was that Morgan was thirty-two now and he'd started to lose a yard of pace...

So, the first time he was one on one with Morgan, Jamie knocked the ball past him and took him on.

Jamie screamed past Morgan. It was as if they were two different species. Jamie's pace was frightening. Only his mis-control on the byline stopped him from getting in a cross. But he'd already shown what he could do.

"Watch yourself," Morgan sniped into Jamie's ear as they jogged back into position. Then Morgan turned his head to the side, covered one of his nostrils with his thumb and blew out a load of snot from his other nostril.

The clear, phlegmy liquid landed on Jamie's boot. Jamie could have sworn Morgan had done it on purpose. He stood and stared at Morgan. What was his problem?

Jamie had heard that you weren't supposed to take the mickey out of senior players in training, but that wasn't what he was doing. He was just playing his normal game. If that happened to make Morgan look like a fool, well, that was his problem. Not Jamie's.

Jamie only knew one thing: he would never have a better opportunity to impress Brian Robertson. He had to show him every skill he had in his locker.

So, the next time Jamie got the ball, he did a double step-over. His feet were lightning quick as they flashed over the ball.

However, by now, Rick Morgan had had enough. He swiped his foot violently through both Jamie and the ball, leaving Jamie in a crumpled heap on the ground.

Jamie's shin was racked with pain. He tried to get up, but he could only put his weight on one leg.

This was getting serious now.

"Oi, Wolf! He's only a kid!" shouted Dave Lewington as he sprinted to stand between the feuding players.

"And the kid needs to learn some respect," snorted Morgan, spitting out of his mouth now. This time he just missed Jamie's face.

"Not my fault you're too slow!" Jamie snapped as he got back to his feet.

Morgan pushed Dave Lewington out of the way to stand face to face with Jamie.

"Who do you think you are, coming on to our pitch and giving me your lip, you little runt?" he raged. "You're with the big boys now... Do you know the pain I can cause you?"

On the sidelines, Tommy Taylor put his whistle in his mouth and was just about to blow. He didn't want the kid to get massacred before he'd even played a game for the club.

But, just as he was about to blow, Brian Robertson raised his hand silently in the air as if to say: *Just wait a second*.

Back on the pitch, Jamie's pulse was beginning to race. He'd been in this position before. People had always tried to bully him on the football pitch. It was their only way of stopping him.

Jamie didn't care how famous or rich Rick Morgan was; he was still a bully, and if Jamie had learned one thing, it was that you have to show bullies you're not scared of them.

Even if it meant pretending.

"Yeah," said Jamie. "Shame you ain't quick enough to catch me then, innit!"

Then Jamie jogged away. He could feel his body shaking, pumping adrenaline around his veins in case this turned into a real fight. He just hoped that wouldn't happen. It would be a terrible way to end his first training session with the Foxborough team.

"You'll get yours," Jamie heard Rick say in a cold, threatening tone behind him. "Trust me, you'll get yours."

Out on the touchline, Tommy Taylor took the whistle out of his mouth and nodded to Brian Robertson.

"The kid's got guts, hasn't he, gaffer?" he said.

"Oh, he can stand up for himself, all right, Tommy."

Then an idea seemed to pop into Brian Robertson's head.

"How old did you say he was again, Tommy?"

⑬
Bunking Off

Jamie was just leaving the First Team dressing room when he heard his name being called out.

"Jamie!" yelled Dave Lewington. "It's my birthday tonight. Alfredo's. Eight-thirty. See you there."

Jamie almost swallowed his tongue. This was just getting better and better. First training, now they wanted him to go out with them!

"Cool," nodded Jamie. "And happy birthday!"

The Butcher and Bolt spent the whole journey to school asking Jamie how training with the First Team had been. It was something they were all desperate to do and now Jamie had done it.

The only word he'd been able to find to describe it

was "amazing". He didn't even have time to tell them about his run-in with Rick Morgan, or the fact that he'd been invited to Dave Lewington's birthday, before they arrived at the school gates.

As Xabi and Bolt got out at the entrance to Compton High School, they turned around to see where Jamie was. He was still sitting in Hassan's car.

"Come on, Jamie, you're going to be late for maths!" yelled Bolt.

"Nah, I'm not coming to school today, guys," said Jamie, closing the door. "Got to talk business with my dad. Don't tell the teachers that, though!"

As Hassan sped away, Jamie looked back at his housemates walking into school. They had always seen it differently to Jamie.

If he was honest, Jamie didn't see the point of school much these days. He'd hardly done any work since he'd joined Compton last year. He was going to be a footballer anyway, so what was the point in maths and all those other lessons? Wouldn't he be better off working on his skills?

And today of all days, it would have seemed extra strange; going from sharing a dressing room with a team of football superstars to sitting in a classroom, listening to some boring teacher.

But Xabi and Bolt were completely the opposite.

They'd never missed a day of school since they'd started at Foxborough. Bolt, in particular, seemed to actually enjoy school. Jamie had never seen that done before!

One evening, back at Mrs L's, when Jamie was playing on the computer and Bolt was reading a book, Jamie had actually asked, "Oi, Bolt. So how come you're so into school and reading and all that stuff?"

Bolt had taken off his glasses and looked at Jamie, half as though he thought Jamie was stupid for asking the question and half as though he felt sorry for Jamie for not knowing the answer.

"Power," he'd replied, prodding his glasses back up his nose to carry on reading. "Knowledge is power."

"Oh, right, yeah," said Jamie, nodding vigorously. He didn't have a clue what Bolt was talking about.

Match Report

Jamie was in one of the best moods of his life as he walked back into the Travelodge for the business meeting with his dad. He couldn't keep the smile from his face.

He loved the fact that he was sharing all this with his dad, too. It was bringing them so much closer together. They were partners now. Partners in Jamie's football future.

"Ah, it's the star of the newspapers, eh?" said Ian Reacher as Jamie sat down opposite him in the hotel restaurant. Jamie noticed his dad was already halfway through his lunch.

"I know," said Jamie, squirming with embarrassment. "Sorry about that, Dad. I had no idea they were going to do that whole WAG story. And how did they find out about me changing my name?"

Jamie thought for a second. This had been on his mind for the last few weeks. And he hoped it would make his dad happy…

"You know, Dad," he mumbled. "I *could* change my name back … now that we're—"

"Oh, forget all that stuff, Jamie! This publicity is great for us. If we can get you into the front pages as well as the back ones, it opens up whole new markets for fans and sponsorship deals. Takes us into a completely different league. Just make sure you hang on to that bird, eh!"

"Her name's Jack."

"It's great for the brand, Jamie. The papers are lapping it up. And if you're going to dump her, make sure you only do it if you've got another cracker lined up!"

"Dad, I'm not going to—"

"Trust me, Jamie, these lifestyle mags will kill for a *Jamie Johnson at home with his childhood sweetheart* set of pics. In fact, I'll make a few calls, see if I can get a bidding war going."

"But I'm not getting my media training until next year, shouldn't I—"

"Too late. The media are interested in you *now*. And it's not just the tabloids, either – have you seen what

Charles Summers has written?"

Jamie's dad passed him the paper. It was one of the posh ones. It seemed to spread over the whole table.

Jamie turned to the sports section. In the bottom right-hand corner of the page was Charles Summers' report from the Youth Cup Final.

Even though Jamie never read the posh papers, he still knew who Charles Summers was. He was the most respected journalist in football. Even some of the Premier League managers listened to what he said.

Jamie started to read the match report and almost immediately his mind flashed back to his old school reports. This felt almost the same. Except football was his best subject.

are just two points clear of the

Young Foxes Devour Harrington
From Charles Summers at The Lair

Youth Cup Final
Foxborough 4 – 1 Harrington Wanderers

The Foxborough Fledglings won their first trophy in such style that there can be little doubt they have the pedigree to make it to the very top of the professional game.

Yet despite the obvious quality of each of Foxborough's youngsters, there was only one name on the lips of the capacity crowd at The Lair last night: Jamie Johnson.

You only had to watch him bound after the ball like a puppy chasing a silver wrapper in the wind to see that this boy was born to play football. Did he come out of his mother's stomach dribbling a ball?

And who better to guide Johnson along the road to football glory than Brian Robertson? Now there's a manager who knows a thing or two about winning trophies...

Jamie handed the paper back to his dad. He still didn't like reading the big papers.

"Looks all right," he said. In truth, he hadn't understood half of it, and he certainly didn't like being compared to a dog. But overall, it seemed pretty positive.

"All right?!" his dad said. He was looking at Jamie as though he were mad.

"Have you got any idea what this article is worth to us? What with all this publicity and the little favour that Esther did me last night by mentioning that we hadn't agreed a deal yet... I reckon the last twenty-four hours have just put another ten-thousand pounds on your contract, just like that," he said, clicking his fingers. "And I'm talking a week, by the way!"

Jamie had never been great with numbers. The only thing he did know was that his stomach needed some food. He picked up the menu.

"I'm starving," he said. "By the way, I trained with the First Team today."

"The First Team? Are you serious?" his dad said, ripping the menu from Jamie's hands. His eyes were wild.

"A fifteen-year-old training with Foxborough's First Team? Well, this is it, then! This is when we strike. Tomorrow, I'll tell the chairman that we've had interest from clubs abroad and unless they match those offers, we'll be off!"

"Abroad? But I've only just joined Foxborough!"

"First rule of business, Jamie – never accept the opening offer. I'm just flushing them out... Them knowing there's other interest means they'll have to up their offer. They'll have to... There's no way they could have you leaving to join another club."

Jamie's dad wiped his mouth with his serviette. Then he scrunched it up into a little ball and chucked it on to his empty plate. Jamie could see he was getting more and more excited as he talked.

"Then, once we get your deal signed, I'll be able to set up an office ... get other clients. This is just the start – you'll see," he beamed.

Jamie's dad's eyes glazed over for a second. Then his concentration was back on Jamie.

"Anyway, enough about me. Do you know what you want?"

Jamie had a think. Different images presented themselves in his mind. A house. Maybe one with a home cinema ... or a swimming pool... New clothes... A car!

"How much is a Bentley?" he asked. "I think I'd quite like one of them when I'm old enough to drive."

"What?!" his dad said, looking at Jamie with an

incredulous expression on his face.

"You asked me what I wanted. I think I'd like a Bentley or maybe a 4 x 4."

"I meant for lunch, you idiot!"

Jamie's chicken and rice had only just arrived when his dad started drumming his fingers on the table and looking at his watch.

Then he drained his cup of coffee and stood up.

"How much cash have you got on you, Jamie?" he asked, putting on his jacket.

Jamie rummaged through his wallet. He still had a couple of notes and some coins left from the money Mike had sent up to him.

"Erm, I've got a few—"

"Great. You settle this one," he said, handing Jamie the bill. "I've got to go and meet some kit sponsors. Let's see what offers they're going to put on the table to be associated with a fifteen-year-old prodigy! I'll call you later."

As he left, he scrunched Jamie's shoulder with the palm of his hand.

"Well done today," he said. "We're really close now. Really close."

15
Hanging Up

"Yuck! You stink, and you're Eggyboff now!" shouted Bolt, chucking a mini-football at Xabi, who caught it and threw it back twice as hard.

Eggyboff was a game the Foxborough boys played all the time. It was a bit like It or Dare. One person would set the challenge, such as: "Next one to speak is Eggyboff!" and that would be it – silence for hours on end! Because being Eggyboff was worse than anything else. It was like having the worst lurgy in the world!

It had actually got really serious once when, at the beginning of an academy game, one of the Foxborough players had shouted: "Next one to touch the ball is Eggyboff!" All the Foxborough players were so desperate to avoid being Eggyboff that they allowed the opposition striker to dribble past the whole team and roll the ball into the net! Steve Brooker was so angry he almost had a fit!

"Oi, guys, can you keep it down for a sec? I'm trying to read an email!" said Jamie, a little more rudely than he had meant to.

"Ooooh," Xabi said, "sorr-eee!! Is this to do with your big 'business meeting', then?"

"No!" said Jamie. "Anyway – I'm not talking to you! You're Eggyboff!"

Xabi kicked the mini sponge football straight at Jamie. It hit him smack in the face. No wonder Xabi was the free-kick taker.

Jamie shook his head and put on his headphones. At least that way he wouldn't be able to hear them while he read the email. It was from Mike.

Mike was Jamie's main man. Although he was actually Jamie's granddad, he'd been more like Jamie's dad when he was growing up.

Football was their common bond. Mike had actually played for Hawkstone United, their local team, and had been set for a brilliant career only for an injury – torn cruciate ligaments – to end his playing days. That was why it meant so much to him to see Jamie following in his footsteps.

From: Mike
Cc:
Subject: GLORY

Attachments: *none*

Verdana 12 **B** *I* U T

Jamie! I've just finished watching the game and I'm now over at your mum's sending this email. [In fact this is your mum typing for him, Jamie – he loves email now and thinks I'm his secretary! He says he wants to go on Facebook next! X]

Anyway, I'm giving you 9 ½ out of 10 tonight. You were brilliant, boy! The way you attacked your man and took your goal was fantastic! ☺

Make sure you always play with the freedom you showed tonight, JJ. This game is about glory. Don't let anyone ever tell you otherwise!

I'll stop rambling on now, but I want you to know that you are already a better footballer than I ever was. It's true! In fact, I reckon you're already good enough to play in the Premier League. I can see you shaking your head but I mean it, JJ! No one's got what you've got.

My prediction is you'll fire one into the top corner on your debut! The whole ground will stand and clap you, and I'll be standing taller than anyone else!

I'm so proud of you, JJ.

See you soon,

Mike

P.S. I wanted to give you 10 out of 10 but, as my coaches at Hawkstone used to tell me, there's always room for improvement, even in the best player in the world.

P.P.S. If you do make your debut this season, try not to make it against the Hawks, will you? We're doing badly enough as it is! We don't need you getting us relegated!

** Bye from Mum and Jeremy too and congrats on winning your goal! ☺ ☺ Xx

Jamie smiled as he logged out. It was amazing how a father and daughter could be so different. Mike was a legend and had taught Jamie everything he knew about football. And his daughter (Jamie's mum) still hadn't worked out that you *scored* a goal, not *won* a goal!

Jamie's phone was ringing. It was Jack. He decided to take the call out in the landing so he could get a bit more privacy.

"Oooh! Private conversation for Jamie boy," Xabi teased. "Is that your new mate, Dave Lewington?"

Jamie had told them about his dinner invite when they'd got back from school. Bolt was genuinely excited for him but Xabi seemed to be a bit envious of all the attention Jamie was suddenly getting.

"What's the Spanish for 'jealousy will get you nowhere'?" Jamie joked and closed the door behind him.

"Is that my *WAG*?" Jamie teased, answering the phone.

"Oh God, that was so embarrassing," laughed Jack. "They wouldn't stop going on about it at school today!"

"I know – same here at training!" smiled Jamie. "It's mad, innit?"

"Yeah. I don't care about all that stuff, though. I'm just looking forward to seeing you. When are you back, JJ?"

"Well, I kind of need to talk to you about—"

"Do you want to watch a DVD tonight? Or go out somewhere?"

"Listen, Jack, I'm really sorry but I'm not going to be able to come back tonight."

Jack's silence made Jamie feel uncomfortable. He hated giving her bad news.

"But you said if you won—"

"I know, but then everything changed today. I've just trained with the First Team! And they've invited me out to Dave Lewington's birthday tonight and, well, you know..."

"'You know' what? What are you trying to say, Jamie?"

The beeps on Jamie's phone indicated he had a call waiting.

"One second, Jack," said Jamie. "I've got another call coming through – I better take it."

"Fine!" said Jack. She wasn't happy.

The other call was Jamie's dad.

"It's all starting to happen, Jamie," he said. "I've got a meeting with the Foxborough chairman tomorrow – they're going to increase their offer!"

"Wicked," said Jamie. "Erm, Dad, can I call you b—"

But his dad had already gone.

Jamie reconnected to Jack.

"Sorry about that, Jack, just contract business I had to discuss with Dad... Listen ... tonight ... it's just, well, it's the whole Foxborough squad. And they've asked me to go."

"When *are* you coming back, anyway? On Saturday?"

"I could do, but by the time I've got home it'll be late and then I'll have to leave again on Sunday so there's not really much point—"

"Not much point? Thanks very much, Jamie!"

"All right, well, you can always come up here, can't you? I'll take you shopping. Once I sign this contract, Dad says we'll be loaded. Then we can buy loads of—"

"Jamie! I've got my exams!"

"Yeah – and I've got my football!"

There was a long pause.

"Look, babe—"

"Don't call me 'babe'!" Jack snapped.

"OK, look, I'm sorry ... but I'll make it up to you. When I turn pro I'll get invited to all the premieres and that stuff and you can come with me!"

"HEL-LO! Jamie, can we get back to the real world, please? You still don't get it, do you? I don't care about that rubbish! I'm not interested in being your *WAG*! I'm a person, you know?"

"But Dad says it's good for me to have a WAG, for

72

the magazines and ev—"

"Well, he can go and find you one then, can't he?!"

Then the phone went dead. Jamie looked at his handset. Jack's name went a paler colour on his screen. Then it disappeared.

Jack had hung up. She'd just broken up with him.

Text Alert

Jamie stepped out of the shower and grabbed a towel. Then he looked at himself in the mirror.

The three boys had drawn a target zone in the corner of the glass where they pussed all their spots. The aim was to get the pus to go right in the centre of the target zone. They knew it was disgusting but they found it funny. They'd even asked Mrs Luscombe not to clean that area!

Jamie inspected his chin but, for once, he had no spots at all! He smiled as he spiked up his hair with gel.

As he got into the cab to head to Alfredo's, Jamie checked his phone to see if there was a text or missed call from Jack. But there was nothing.

Jamie was actually a bit surprised that he didn't feel

more upset about breaking up with her. Maybe he should have been crying or something. But the truth was, right now, Jamie felt more excited than depressed. Tonight he was going out with some of the most famous footballers in the country.

Sure he would miss Jack, of course he would. But he also knew that if he wanted to find a girl to replace her, it shouldn't be too hard. He was a footballer now, after all.

When they arrived, Jamie got out of the cab and gave the driver some money. He checked his reflection one last time in the car window. Then he went inside.

Walking into the restaurant, Jamie felt a flutter of nerves. He hoped he wouldn't say the wrong thing and make a fool of himself tonight. He just wanted to be accepted.

"Jamie!" shouted Dave Lewington. "Over here, mate. Just in time. We're about to order."

Jamie sat down and took off his jacket. For some reason he felt boiling hot. He looked around him. The walls of the restaurant were covered with signed photographs of the Foxborough players. There was even one of the squad in the restaurant with the Premier League trophy! They must have come here when they won the title last season.

Jamie picked up the menu only to find that the whole

thing was in Italian! He didn't have a clue what to do. He could point to a dish at random, he reckoned, but what if it was something he hated, like an olive salad?

"Ah, Mr Dave!" said a big, fat man as he embraced Dave Lewington with a super-sized hug. "Anda happy birthday to youa!"

"Thanks, Alberto. How's business?" Dave enquired.

"Oh, very good, sir. Very good indeed. The usual for everybody?"

"Yes, please, Alberto, that will be great."

"No problem, Mr Dave. You know whatever you want, you just ask Alfredo!"

And, with a hearty laugh, Alberto instructed his team of young waitresses to collect the menus. Jamie breathed a sigh of relief. Who knows what he would have ended up ordering if it had been left up to him!

Almost immediately, a selection of every starter under the sun appeared on the table.

Garlic bread, smoked salmon, melon, prawns, cold meats, spare ribs, sardines and tomato salad all seemed to appear out of nowhere. Jamie quickly realized that he was completely stuffed and they had only had the starters!

It was at around nine-thirty p.m. that a strange ritual occurred right in front of Jamie. Seemingly as one, all the First Team players reached for their mobile phones, read a text message and then put their phones back in their pockets without even bothering to respond.

Jamie wondered what all the texts were and why not one of them had sent a reply.

Then, a couple of minutes later, Jamie felt his own phone vibrate in his pocket. Discreetly, he reached into his jacket. He assumed it would be from Jack but, when he opened his inbox, he saw that it was from a number he didn't recognize.

Slowly, Jamie pressed the button to open the message.

.ıll ⬜ 🔺
✉ Messages
07555 212 333
You are in the First Team squad to play Holton on Sunday. The coach for the airport leaves at 1 p.m. We'll be travelling in tracksuits. Anne
Options   Reply   Menu

Jamie's hand was shaking. He read the message five or six times. At first he thought it might have been a wind-up from Bolt and Xabi. Maybe they had borrowed someone else's phone to try and fool him? But even they wouldn't know that the First Team Administrator was called Anne. Jamie only knew that himself because he'd heard Steve Brooker talking to her on the phone last week to arrange tickets for a First Team game.

This was real. This was serious. This was happening.

Jamie was in Foxborough's First Team squad!

The Next Big Thing

Practically as soon as the Foxborough players had finished their meal, they were surrounded by fans and autograph hunters.

"Excuse me, could we get our photo taken with you?" asked a couple of girls. They were both fit.

"Sure you can," Rick Morgan grinned, sleazily.

He stood up proudly and put his arms around the girls. As Morgan smiled, Jamie noticed how his long, sharpened teeth resembled fangs. Suddenly, he realized why Morgan was called Wolf.

"No," one of the girls said. "Not with *you*! With Jamie! Our brothers say he's going to be the next big thing!"

Rick Morgan's lip curled with anger.

"Of course you can," said Jamie.

He loved the fact that he was already more popular than Rick Morgan and he hadn't even made his First Team debut yet!

It was about ten-thirty when Dave Lewington called Alberto over to settle the bill.

"Oh, no, Mr Dave – it is your birthday! On the house!"

It was strange, Jamie thought, how it was always the really rich people who got given things for free.

As the Foxborough players left the restaurant, Jamie was starting to feel tired. He knew he should get an early night. After all, he was in the squad for Sunday's game. There was a chance he could make his Premier League debut!

"I'm off, Dave. Cheers for inviting me," Jamie said, shaking his captain's hand as the players exited the restaurant. "I'll see you on the coach tomorrow."

"Are you in the squad? Nice one!" said Dave. He seemed genuinely pleased for Jamie. "You should celebrate. Come out with us tonight, mate. We'll get you in, no problem."

"Thanks," said Jamie, crossing the road. "But I'd better get back."

"Yeah, he's just a little boy!" Rick Morgan suddenly shouted. Jamie could hear the jealousy that laced

Morgan's taunt. "Go home, little boy. Go back to your mummy."

Jamie's blood boiled. What was Rick's problem? Jamie's career was just beginning and Rick's was near the end. Why couldn't he just accept that?

Fine, Jamie thought to himself. *Now he's said that, I* will *go out with them, just to annoy him!*

Jamie turned around and ran back across the road to rejoin the other players.

But he didn't look before he ran. So he didn't see the car coming.

The collision took place in an instant.

And then everything went dark.

The Results

Jamie opened his eyes. His vision was blurry. There was a torch. Someone was shining a torch in his eyes. He was in a room with white walls.

"Is he OK? Can he hear us?"

Jamie recognized the voice but was engulfed by a wave of tiredness. He fell back into a deep sleep.

"Hello, Jamie, how are you feeling?" The nurse smiled at Jamie as he woke up. She had a nice smile.

Jamie nodded. Every bone in his body hurt. It felt as though he had been sawn into a hundred different pieces and then stuck back together again.

He looked down at his left leg. It was in plaster and hoisted into the air.

Jamie looked at his surroundings. A hospital room with flowers and lots of "get well soon" cards. He didn't know what day it was or how long he had been here.

"What happened?" Jamie asked.

Jamie's mind frantically scampered into the past to find some answers. There were some corners of light: being out with his teammates … crossing the road. But nothing else. The rest was just empty shadows.

There was silence in the room. Nobody answered Jamie's question. He looked at his mum. She smiled weakly and looked to the floor.

"Finally!" said Jamie when the doctor entered his room, carrying with him an envelope of X-rays. "I've been stuck here for days now!"

"I'm sorry to have kept you waiting, Jamie," said the doctor. His voice was soft and calm. "I realize it must have been frustrating."

"Frustrating … I can't feel a thing because of these drugs and every day I'm losing my fitness. It's more than frustrating! How long am I out for, doc? If I don't get back soon, Brian Robertson will go out and buy another winger and I'll have blown my chance. I've been training with the First Team, you know!"

"Jamie, the first thing to state is that you have

sustained very significant injuries. Your back was severely injured by the initial impact of the collision, while your left leg was broken in three places. We believe this occurred when you landed on the ground, by which time you were already unconscious and therefore unable to break the weight of your fall.

"We have inserted three screws into your leg to hold the bone in place, but that is a perfectly normal procedure, and I am pleased to say that that operation was a complete success—"

"Great!" said Jamie. "Nice one!"

"As for your back," continued the doctor, "you were extremely lucky, Jamie. Had your spine collapsed, you would have been paral—"

"So when will I be back in training again, doc?" Jamie asked again. "Just give me a date ... something to work to..."

"Jamie," said the doctor, taking off his glasses and resting them on the table. "I'm not sure that you fully understand the gravity of your injuries. You are extremely fortunate that you will be able to walk again..."

Part TWO
Six months later

⑲

A Bad Dream

Saturday 28 November

Jamie lifted the crisp packet above his mouth and tipped what was left down his throat. Some of the crumbs missed and found new homes either on his chin or his jumper.

He wiped the back of his hand across his chin and licked it. Then he licked his fingers clean.

That was the only benefit from the fact that his career was over – he could eat whatever he wanted. He'd put on a load of weight, but it didn't matter. He had nothing to be fit for and no one to look good for.

He looked at his watch: 11.04 p.m. He knew he should probably go to bed or at least have a shower to clean himself up but instead he flicked through all the TV channels again. Then he got up to see what else was in the fridge.

Jamie had been home for five months. Coming back had been the weirdest feeling Jamie had ever experienced. Everything was exactly the same – his room had not been touched since the day he'd left for Foxborough. Nothing at all had changed. Except that everything had changed – for Jamie.

He'd left this house with hope and expectation – his whole future as a footballer was ahead of him. And yet he'd returned with nothing.

The moment that car had ripped into Jamie's fragile body, his whole world had exploded.

Just after midnight, Jamie finally turned off the TV. Even he couldn't watch any more; he was starting to go cross-eyed. He traipsed up the stairs and got undressed.

He examined the scars on his left leg. It was strange to think that his bones were being held in place by a set of screws. What would happen if they went rusty? And would he set off the security checks at airports for the rest of his life?

Jamie lay in his bed, looking at the old Hawkstone United posters on his bedroom wall. He could still remember putting them all up. He'd dreamed that one day he'd play for the Hawks, just like Mike had.

Jamie turned over. Now, when he was actually *in* bed, he wasn't tired at all; his eyes were wide open.

All he wanted was for sleep to come and rescue him, transport him to some other place.

But, ever since he'd got back home, his dreams had been a dark forest, haunted by evil shapes and images.

Almost every night, Jamie would dream that he was back in the hospital on the day that Steve Brooker had told him the news. Steve looked like a policeman in a TV soap who is just about to tell someone that a member of their family has died.

"We're going to let you go, Jamie," he'd confessed.

"What?! But I can make it back, Steve. I promise you. I'll be able to walk again in two months and then, when I start jog—"

"It's out of my hands, Jamie. Look, by the time you get out of plaster, all the muscle tissue in your legs will have wasted away. We can't keep you on in that state. It could be months before you could even kick a ball again."

"But Steve, you know me, you know I never give up—"

"Look, if you do make some miraculous recovery, you can always call me. You know where I am."

"Steve, I'm begging you … don't do this!"

"I'm sorry, Jamie. I really am. It's such bad luck – you

know how much I rated you... But you have to accept that it's over."

Sometimes, Jamie woke up shouting Steve's name. For a second, he'd hope that the last few months had all been some terrible nightmare and that he was really back at Mrs Luscombe's house with Xabi and Bolt...

But it wasn't a nightmare. It was worse than that. This was real.

Bolt From the Past

Sunday 20 December

Jamie dialled the number again.

It must have been the hundredth time he'd dialled it since the accident. For the first couple of days, when he'd tried to call from the hospital, Jamie's dad's phone had just rung out. Jamie thought his dad would be worried about him, not knowing where he was.

But, after a week or so, when the message changed to "The number you called has not been recognized. Please check the number and try again," Jamie started to understand what was really happening.

With each passing day, Jamie could feel his rage

starting to bubble over. But Jamie was even more angry with himself than with his dad. How could he have allowed himself to be fooled so easily? He had been an idiot to believe that his dad had actually cared about *him* and not just the money.

Never again, Jamie pledged to himself. Never again.

Wednesday 20 January

Jamie had to flick through practically all of the satellite channels on his TV to find it. And even when he did, the picture quality was terrible. It looked as though the match was being played on another planet, not just another continent.

"Welcome to Angola for the opening match in the African Nations Cup, as the hosts take on Ghana," said the commentator.

Jamie could easily tell that the commentator was actually sitting in a studio somewhere in Europe watching the game on TV, just like everyone else.

The reason that Jamie was so keen to watch this game was that Ghana had called up a sixteen-year-old striker to make his international debut. He was six foot two and as fast as lightning. And his nickname was Bolt.

Jamie got a big bag of popcorn and settled down to

watch the game. It was the first match he'd watched since the accident.

"Go on! Give it to Bolt!" Jamie roared, pelting popcorn at the screen. "He's a goal machine!"

And, very quickly, Jamie was proved right. Bolt didn't just score one goal. He scored a hat-trick – two bullet headers and a bicycle kick. Not bad for a sixteen-year-old!

As he watched Bolt being carried off the pitch by the Ghana fans, who'd draped their striker in the national flag, Jamie felt so proud of his old room-mate.

For once, his body felt as if it had some energy. Jamie stood up and picked up his old sponge football. Then he tossed it into the air.

He managed to do four kick-ups before he lost control and smashed his foot into the table. It was seriously painful. But what hurt more than the physical pain was the fact that Jamie had only been able to do four kick-ups.

His record was three hundred and eighty-four.

Friday Night

Friday 22 January

It was a Friday night and Jamie was sitting at home, bored.

His mum and Jeremy had gone out for their anniversary dinner, but Jamie didn't see why they should be the only ones to get a treat. He decided to go down to the shop to get himself some ice cream.

He got some money together – he was rapidly running out, soon he'd have to ask his mum if he could borrow some more – and chucked on his hoodie.

When he got to the shop, Jamie headed straight for the ice-cream freezer. He was just choosing which flavour to get when he sensed that two girls standing by the till were talking about him. They were whispering and smirking.

Jamie felt his body tighten. It always made him nervous when he thought people were talking about him.

Then the embarrassing sound of the ringtone on Jamie's phone seemed to bellow out of his pocket. It was a song that had been in the charts ages ago. It made Jamie look way out of date.

He quickly got his phone out and switched it to silent. It was only Mike, anyway. Jamie would call him back tomorrow.

Jamie gave it a couple more minutes. Then he walked up to the cash register and plonked his tub of ice cream down on the counter.

"Excuse me," said one of the girls, sliding over to him. "You used to be Jamie Johnson, yeah?"

Jamie laughed and slipped his hood off.

"Yeah," he said. "I still am!"

He was happy. He hadn't been recognized in ages. He picked up the pen on the counter ready to sign some autographs.

"What's happened to you?" said the girl closest to him. Her face was covered with disgust.

"Yeah," said the other girl. "You used to be fit. Sort yourself out, mate!"

Jamie couldn't even respond. He was shocked. And seriously embarrassed.

As he watched the girls leave the store, he pulled his

hood back up and tugged it as far over his face as he could.

"Is that everything?" said the store assistant, beeping the ice cream through.

"What?" said Jamie. "Oh. Yeah. That's all."

(22)
The Phone Call

Saturday 23 January

It was one in the afternoon and Jamie was still in bed. He was deciding whether or not to watch the Hawkstone game on TV.

Hawkstone were right near the bottom of the table. There was a serious danger they could get relegated this season. But, even though it was a huge match for them, Jamie still wasn't sure whether he could be bothered to watch it.

He was just channel-hopping when Jeremy barged into his room without knocking.

He looked at the state of Jamie's floor, covered in

dirty clothes, crisp wrappers and old newspapers.

"This place is an absolute tip, clean it up!" he demanded. "And what's this about you asking your mum for more money? What's happened to your savings?"

That really annoyed Jamie. Why did his mum have to discuss *everything* with Jeremy? It was as if, since they'd got married, she'd lost the ability to have her own opinion about anything.

As always, Jamie would have to fight the battle on his own.

"What do you think's happened to it?" he snapped back. "I spent it, didn't I?"

"Can I ask you a question, Jamie?" said Jeremy, standing over Jamie's bed, his face reddening with anger. "School starts in September, right? Do you plan to spend the next eight months watching TV or are you actually going to get off your backside and do something?"

"I'll do what I want!" barked Jamie. "You've got no idea about me or my life. Do you even understand how good I was? You don't know anything!"

The phone was ringing in the other room but neither of them answered it. They just kept on shouting at each other. Until they heard Jamie's mum scream.

*

Mike Johnson had had a massive heart attack.

His neighbour had found him on the kitchen floor while, in the other room, the Hawkstone game was still blaring on the TV.

Mike had been rushed to hospital but, by the time he'd got there, it was too late. The only good thing, the doctors had said, was that it was all so quick that Mike wouldn't have suffered too much pain.

The next few hours were a blur of misery. The only person who was able to hold it together was Jeremy. He was the one who made all the calls, who did all the organizing, who made sure Jamie and his mum had something to eat.

Jamie was completely numb. His brain couldn't process what had happened. It wasn't true. It couldn't have been. Mike had called him only yesterday. Twenty-four hours ago...

Mike had been the one person who'd been there for Jamie. Always.

And now he was gone.

One New Message

Sunday 24 January

Jamie was alone in his bedroom the next day when he finally made himself listen to it.

He knew he had to do it sometime and, in a sense, he wanted to. But he also knew it would be one of the most painful things he would ever do.

He called the voicemail on his phone.

"You have one new message. To listen to your messages, press one. First new message left on Friday, January twenty-second, at 8.49 p.m."

Then Mike's voice came on. He sounded a bit down but he was making an effort to be cheerful for Jamie:

"Hiya, JJ, only me. I was just wondering if you wanted to come and watch the Hawks game with me tomorrow. It's a big one! They need our support! If we lose tomorrow, I reckon they should just give the job to Harry Armstrong; he couldn't do any worse than this lot!

"Maybe see you tomorrow, then. But don't worry if you can't… I'm sure you've got lots on.

"I'll stop rambling on now, but give me a call sometime when you've got a second, JJ… You've been so quiet since you got back… I miss you, mate…"

And that was the end of the message.

Jamie took in a massive gulp of air. The woman on voicemail was asking Jamie whether he wanted to delete the message. Jamie would never do that. He pressed *save*. He would keep it for ever.

Out of the corner of his eye, Jamie saw his mum walk past his room. Then she stopped and came in, slowly putting something down on his bookshelf. Neither of them said a word.

"Mum … can I have a hug?" Jamie suddenly asked.

"Of course," she said, opening her arms wide.

Jamie clasped his arms around her and hugged as hard as he could.

"I love you, Mum," he mumbled, almost nervously. He wondered why it took such a bad thing to happen for him to be able to say it.

"I love you too, Jamie. You know you're the most important thing in the whole world to me, don't you?"

Jamie nodded. His heart was throbbing in his throat.

"And I'm not the only one who adored you," she said, turning to pick up the book that she had laid on top of the bookshelf when she came in.

"Mike wanted you to have this," she said, handing it to Jamie.

"What is it?" asked Jamie.

"It's his diary."

Jamie sat down on his bed and opened the diary at the beginning.

Jamie's Second Birthday
I was lucky enough to spend the whole day with my gift of a grandson. When I look at him, when I am in his happy, cheerful presence, it's as if someone switches on a light in my life. He is my reason for being alive.

Jamie shut his eyes to try and hold in his emotions. Then he turned the page.

Gave Jamie his first football today. OK, so he's only three and a half but you can never be too young. It was quite amazing, too. His eyes seemed to sparkle as he took the ball from my hands. And stone me, somehow (maybe the Johnson genes!) the boy seemed to know what to do with it!

He put the ball on the floor and wandered across the room, prodding it forward. He looks like he's going to be a left-footer.

The only time he got upset was when I tried to take the ball back off him. So I didn't.

Jamie touched the pages of the diary as softly, as tenderly as he could. He wanted the tips of his fingers to connect with the ink that had come from the pen that Mike had once held in his hand.

As he read and touched Mike's words, for the briefest of moments, Jamie felt Mike's presence surround him.

Went to watch Jamie play for his school team for the first time today. They had some decent players. But none of them were like Jamie. The way he opens up his body and assesses his options before he even receives the ball... He's different. Special...

When we got home, all he wanted to do was talk about my career with Hawkstone. I showed him my Young Player of the Year trophies and told him about my best games before my injury. I think he's starting to love the Hawks as much as I do! Imagine if he plays for them one day! He's already got more skill than I ever had!

He has no idea how fantastic it makes me feel when he asks me questions about my life. I'm so proud of that boy. He's had it tough with his dad but he still has such a positive way about everything he does. I hope the world is kind to him.

Jamie slowly closed the diary. Then, for the first time in months, for the first time since the accident, he did what he most needed to do. He cried.

Back to Sunningdale

Wednesday 27 January

It had been so long that Jamie almost couldn't find it. But then he spotted it, beneath the huge oak tree that looked naked now, without its leaves.

Jamie sat down on his favourite bench in Sunningdale Park. He looked at the football pitches in front of him. Then he closed his eyes and allowed all the memories of the games he'd played here crash like a tidal wave around his mind.

"Thought I might find you here," called a familiar voice.

Jamie looked up and he couldn't believe his eyes. He couldn't believe who it was.

Jack looked even prettier than the last time he'd seen her. She was just wearing jeans and a T-shirt but she still looked better than any of the supermodels on TV.

"Can I sit down?" she asked.

"Course," said Jamie, shifting up to make space. "It's as much your bench as it is mine."

They both smiled as they looked at the engraving they'd made years before on the bench, using Jamie's penknife:

J & J 4EVER

They sat in silence for a few moments before Jack said, "I'm so sorry about Mike, Jamie."

"Cheers," said Jamie. "Mike always liked you, you know. He said I should make sure that I hung on to you."

Then Jamie tried to begin the speech he'd rehearsed in his mind so many times over the last few weeks.

"Jack, listen, I'm sorry about … what happened when I was at Foxborough," he began. "I was an idiot. I—"

"Oh, forget about it," she said nonchalantly.

Jamie couldn't believe his luck. He couldn't believe she was making things so easy for him.

"Really?" he beamed.

"Yeah, forget about it," she repeated. "I forgot about it months ago."

"OK, cool … great, so we can be…"

"Friends. Yeah, we'll always be friends, Jamie."

"Friends? Oh, yeah … right… It's just I thought … friends. Yeah … friends."

When they were younger, Jamie and Jack had always sprinted down to Sunningdale from their houses. They'd had races to see who could get there first. Of course Jamie had always won. He had natural pace.

He could have been a professional sprinter if he hadn't loved football so much.

But now they were just walking. Slowly. The doctor had said it would be at least another few weeks before Jamie might be able to start running again.

The sky was a dense white sheet, smothering the sun that lay buried above. Jamie felt as though he hadn't seen the sun in years.

"What am I going to do, Jack?" he suddenly asked. He'd stopped walking.

"What do you mean, JJ?"

Jamie smiled. Jack and Mike were the only people who'd ever called him JJ.

"I mean: what am I going to do without football? Football was my life. Without it, I've got … nothing."

Jamie looked at the ground. His emotions were all jumbled up. He didn't even know if he was making sense.

Then Jack took Jamie's hand softly but firmly into hers. Their hands fitted together as neatly as they always had done.

"So get back into football, then," she said, as though it was the most obvious thing in the world.

25
Archie Fairclough
Thursday 28 January

The rain was beating down so violently on the groundsman's decrepit old shed that Jamie could hardly hear the knock of his fist against the weathered wooden door.

When it finally opened, a man stood in front of him, holding a steaming mug of tea in his huge, rough hands. He had an aggressive expression on his face.

"Hi," smiled Jamie, attempting to hold his nerve. "I'm here about the job."

"What job?" snapped the man impatiently. "We haven't advertised a job."

"I know," nodded Jamie. "But I want one."

*

As the heavy storm continued to pelt down, a fat drop of water snaked its way down Jamie's soaked scalp, tickling his neck as it trickled along its journey.

Jamie didn't flick it away; he was focusing all his attention on the man standing in front of him.

Meanwhile, Archie Fairclough, Hawkstone United's Head Groundsman and Kit Manager, looked the young lad up and down. What had brought him here on a Thursday morning in the pouring rain? Didn't he go to school?

The kid seemed keen enough, and Archie knew that, now more than ever, he could do with an extra pair of hands around the place... But he was always wary of people who came asking for a job at Hawkstone. What were their real motives?

Archie pulled his thumb and his fingers across his chin as his mind edged towards a decision. *Strange*, he thought to himself, *I could have sworn I'd seen this kid somewhere before*.

"There ain't no money in it, if that's what you're after," he grunted. "We're not on footballers' wages, you know... And we might all be out of a job come May anyway, if we end up going down."

"I don't care," the boy responded. "I'm not here for the money. I just want to help."

And what's more, Archie Fairclough could have sworn he was telling the truth.

111

26

Straight Talking

Friday 29 January

"A constructive way to generate an income until he goes back to school" was Jeremy's view of Jamie's new job at Hawkstone.

Although Jamie had no intention of ever going back to school, he'd decided to save that argument for another day.

Now, because Jamie was earning his own money, Jeremy couldn't have a go at him any more. In fact, he was even giving Jamie a lift into the Hawks training ground for his first day at work.

Jamie stared at Jeremy as he drove. He was wearing

his leather driving gloves, checking his rear-view mirror every forty-five seconds. He had the news on the radio. He never ever listened to music in the car. And he always stayed exactly on the speed limit.

Straight, Jamie decided. Straight was the ideal word to describe Jeremy. Everything about him was uniform, in order and unsurprising: his hair, his tie, his neatly polished shoes. Even his voice was boring. Jamie hadn't realized that Jeremy had been talking for the last two minutes. He'd just tuned in for the end of the sermon.

"...and that is why punctuality is so important," Jeremy was saying. "It shows an organized mind."

Jamie rolled his eyes. He wondered if the man had ever taken a risk in his life.

Archie Fairclough probably looked older than he actually was. When Jamie had first seen him, he'd thought that he must have been about seventy. But, having worked with him for just a few hours, Jamie soon realized that the wrinkles he'd taken for age were actually just lines – evidence of the countless days he'd spent out in the open air.

The other feature that struck Jamie about Archie was his strength. With his huge hands, he'd clasp a set of five-a-side goals, raise them above his head and walk the length of the pitch with them. His tattooed biceps bulged through the Hawkstone T-shirt that was his daily uniform.

"All right, Cloughie!" all the Hawkstone First Teamers shouted whenever they saw Archie.

He was pretty much a legend within the club. He'd been the Hawks groundsman for twenty years, and when veteran midfielder Harry Armstrong had been appointed Hawkstone player-manager a few days before, one of the first decisions he'd made was to give Archie a promotion and ask him to sit in the dugout during First Team games.

So now Archie's grand title was Head Groundsman *and* Kit Manager. Jamie's title was simply Archie Fairclough's Assistant.

Familiar Foe

"What's your second name, by the way?" asked Archie as he led Jamie out to the pitches. "I need to let the finance people know all your details so that you get your huge pay packet at the end of the month!"

For some reason this made Archie laugh almost uncontrollably. He was properly cracking up. His mug was shaking so much that the tea was beginning to spill down the side.

"Johnson," said Jamie.

"Johnson, eh?" Archie repeated, studying Jamie closely as he spoke. "You know, there was a great young player at this club once called Mike Johnson – he was playing when I first started supporting Hawkstone. Centre back, he was. As hard as nails. If it hadn't been for his injury, he could have done anything in the game. Tell you what, we could do with a player like him now…"

"Yeah," said Jamie. He could feel the slight salty prickle of a tear in the corner of his eye. "I've heard about Mike Johnson."

"OK," said Archie, changing the subject. "The first thing you can do is take these over to the academy boys."

He was pointing to a crate of energy drinks. "They'll come over and drink them at half-time in their game. And make sure you bring back all the empty cartons."

Jamie nodded and started to lug the crate over towards the academy players. He could feel the hot sweat dripping down inside his tracksuit top. He realized that he had hardly done any exercise at all in the last eight months. He was so unfit.

As soon as he arrived, all the academy players gathered quickly around him, snatching the drinks like a group of prisoners that had been starved of water.

They downed the drinks and then chucked the cartons on the ground beneath them. Not one of them bothered to hand their carton back to Jamie. Or say thanks.

Jamie was just bending down to pick them up when he heard the voice that immediately brought back a torrent of bad memories.

"Johnson – is that you?"

Jamie didn't have to turn around to know who it was. He'd recognize that voice anywhere. It was Dillon Simmonds.

Dillon was by far the worst enemy that Jamie had ever had. They had hated each other since the day Jamie had started at Kingfield School. It was Dillon who had started it – having a go at Jamie for being small and always saying how rubbish Jamie was at football.

Dillon had done some really evil things to Jamie, but Jamie had never let it show that he was upset. He didn't want to give Dillon the satisfaction.

Even when Dillon had pulled one of his worst tricks – stealing Jamie's phone and sending a text to Jamie's mum which simply read: **I want 2 kiss u** – Jamie had still tried to laugh it off. Not that his mum and Jeremy had been too amused…

And now here they were, together again at Hawkstone. Except this time all the chips were stacked in Dillon's favour.

Jamie realized he had to at least pretend to be friendly.

"All right, Dil—"

"Ha ha! I knew it was you! So what happened at Foxborough, then? I thought you were supposed to be the next big thing?!"

"I got—"

"Man, how sad are you?! You're like nothing now. And I almost didn't recognize you 'cos you're so fat! Ha! Ha! Ha!"

He still had that same high-pitched hyena laugh that had tormented Jamie when they were at school.

Dillon jogged back towards his teammates, turning only to chuck his drink carton as far away as possible. He knew Jamie would be the one to have to go and pick it up.

As soon as Jamie got home that night, he went straight into the bathroom and locked the door behind him. He couldn't get Dillon's insults out of his mind.

He struggled to pull his clinging wet tracksuit top over his shoulders and head. When he finally managed it, he tossed the sodden top on to the floor.

As Jamie looked up, his reflection in the mirror gave him a shock. He hadn't studied his body in the mirror for months.

He twisted his white, freckled form from side to side, eyeing every inch of himself in the glass.

He softly patted his belly. Gone was the taut, hard stomach that he'd gained by doing hundreds of sit-ups during his Foxborough days. Instead, here was the flabby result of all the ice cream and chips that he'd tucked away mindlessly during his months as a couch potato.

Jamie traced his hands up his body, towards his chest. He squeezed the loose flesh. He couldn't believe it. He even had the beginning of man boobs!

Dillon was right. Jamie was fat.

He ran his fingers through his thick, spiky hair.

"Right! Time for a change!" he said to himself, with a new determination in his voice.

Then he picked up Jeremy's clippers and began that change.

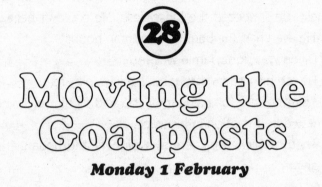

28

Moving the Goalposts

Monday 1 February

"Someone's had a haircut!" said Archie when Jamie got to work on Monday. "But if you wanted to borrow the mower, you only had to ask!"

"What d'you mean?" asked Jamie.

"Oh, doesn't matter," chuckled Archie, his laughter slowly subsiding. "Gaffer says they're playing five-a-side today, so we need to move these goalposts over to that field. Follow me."

Jamie watched as Archie hauled the set of goals above his head and began the arduous trek to the other side of the training ground.

Jamie tried to lift his goals. But they were seriously heavy; Jamie pulled, but he couldn't get them off the ground.

Archie looked around and waved him on impatiently. Jamie didn't know what to do. There was no way he could say he was too weak. This was his job. Somehow, he had to lift these goals.

He bent his knees and crouched down beneath the crossbar. He exhaled a few times, as he'd seen weightlifters do. Then, with a huge push of his lungs and a rush of power through his arms and shoulders, he raised the goals high above his head. A little unsteady at first, he soon found his balance and followed in the direction Archie was heading.

Jamie's whole body ached by the time they reached the training pitch and he and Archie carefully laid the goals down at either end. His thighs, which had taken the brunt of the carrying, were throbbing so hard, it felt as though they might burst through Jamie's tracksuit bottoms.

Jamie breathed out and wrung his wrists to try and get the blood flowing again.

"What?" teased Archie. "You're not out of puff, are you? That was nothing!"

Jamie shook his head. He didn't want Archie to know that that was one of the most gruelling physical tasks he'd ever completed.

"Thanks for that, Cloughie," said a man in a tracksuit, striding purposefully on to the pitch. Jamie instantly knew who the man was. It was Harry Armstrong, the new player-manager of Hawkstone United. Harry had been one of Jamie's favourite players when Jamie was younger.

"No problem, gaffer," said Archie, more cheerful than Jamie had ever seen him before. "We'll come and collect them when training's finished."

"Nice one," said Harry. Then he turned to look at Jamie.

"And I take it this is the new member of staff you've been telling me about, Cloughie?"

"Sure is, gaffer," replied Archie. "He's been with us a couple of weeks now. It's good to have an extra pair of hands around the place."

"Yup – we need all the help we can get at the moment," Harry Armstrong said, stretching out his hand for Jamie to shake. "What did you say your name was again?"

"Jamie, sir … I mean gaffer… I'm Jamie."

They shook hands.

"Welcome to Hawkstone, Jamie," said Armstrong, smiling widely. "Good to have you on board."

The Playmaker

Friday 5 March

Sometimes, on a Friday, as a treat, Archie would let Jamie go and watch the Hawkstone team train ahead of their weekend match.

Jamie loved being so close to the action. Although more than anything else he would have wanted to be out there on the pitch himself, standing as an observer on the touchline gave him an opportunity. He could study the game in a way that wasn't possible when he was in the thick of the action.

For the first time, Jamie was able to analyse the way that football actually worked.

The player Jamie most liked to watch was Glenn Richardson. He was the Hawkstone playmaker and he wore the number ten – the shirt of legends.

Harry Armstrong had said in an interview recently that, if Richardson had been Brazilian, he would have had a hundred caps and been a national hero. And it was certain that, if Hawkstone did end up being relegated, Richardson would be transferred to one of the biggest clubs in the country. He was way too skilful a player not to be playing in the Premier League.

Jamie marvelled at how Richardson could spray fifty-yard through-balls to the striker, each one of them inch-perfect. He could even put backspin on his passes so that they held up enough to prevent the goalkeeper coming out to intercept them.

For a second, Jamie allowed himself to imagine what it would be like playing in the same team as Glenn Richardson: Jamie would stay out on the wing, knowing that Richardson could find him with one of his perfect passes...

But then Jamie stopped himself. He knew that was a painful scab to pick at.

Friday 26 March

"All right, I'm off, Archie," Jamie called into the shed.

As the training ground was empty, he'd mowed every single pitch today. He'd probably walked about five miles in total!

"Did you make sure all the touchlines were completely straight?" asked Archie. He was obsessed with the touchlines. They all had to be exactly perfect.

"Of course!" chuckled Jamie. "See you next week!"

"And where do you think you're going?" said Archie, poking his head out of the shed.

"Home," said Jamie. "I'm done."

"Not quite," said Archie, reaching inside to produce two tins of white paint from one of his cupboards. "I reckon our little shed could do with a lick of paint, don't you?" he smiled. "Especially now that it's an office for two..."

"Ah, come on, Archie," Jamie protested. "It's the weekend and I'm seriously knackered. Can't we do it on Monday?"

"No rest for the wicked, eh?" Archie teased, handing Jamie the brush.

Jamie had no idea that painting a shed could be so tiring. It was seven forty-five by the time he'd finally finished and his arms felt so heavy he didn't know how he was going to carry them home.

"Not bad," said Archie, inspecting the work as Jamie

washed his hands inside the shed. His fingers were almost blue with cold and his pecs ached more than if he'd done two hundred press-ups.

"There you go," said Archie, handing Jamie an envelope.

"What's this?"

"Your wages – you're getting paid this month. But don't worry, I can keep 'em if you don't want 'em!"

"No ... thanks ... I just didn't realize it was the end of the month already."

"Time flies when you're painting sheds, eh," said Archie, laughing heartily at his own joke. "Don't spend it all at once!"

Jamie already knew how he wanted to spend some of it.

30
Knocking on the Door

As soon as Jamie got home, he jumped straight in the shower.

He was in a hurry, but he knew he could do a shower in under thirty seconds…

Then, while he was drying himself, Jamie suddenly noticed something: his belly – it had gone!

Jamie patted his returned six-pack and smiled. Then he tensed his biceps. They were bigger than they had ever been before.

"Thanks, Archie," Jamie laughed as he examined his new muscles in the mirror. "At least all your slave-driving is good for something!"

Jamie put on his best jeans and tucked a wad of money into the pocket. Then he put on some aftershave and went to knock on Jack's door.

As Jamie waited for someone to answer the door, he suddenly realized that he was nervous. He missed Jack a lot. Without her, his life wasn't quite complete…

When Jack opened the door, Jamie was taken aback for a second. He had never seen her wearing glasses before. They really suited her.

"All right?" Jamie opened. "Just wondering if you wanted to go to the cinema tonight? It's on me – I've just been paid!"

"Oh, Jamie, that's really sweet," Jack said, her eyes glistening underneath the security light by her front door. "But we're revising tonight. The exams start next week."

We! Jamie thought. *Who's we?!*

And then, in the background, Jamie saw Alex Marcusfield standing behind Jack. He was holding a bunch of books and he looked really pleased with himself. He even seemed to be smirking at Jamie.

Marcusfield had always been the ugly swot when Jamie was at Kingfield School. But now he didn't look ugly any more and the lucky gimp was getting to spend the whole evening with Jack!

Jamie was so jealous that he wanted to storm into the house, wrestle Marcusfield to the floor, and tell him that Jack was taken and that he should keep his hands OFF!

But he knew that wouldn't impress Jack.

So, the only thing Jamie could do was try to hide his disappointment and say, "Cool... Yeah, I'm pretty busy tonight, anyway. Maybe some other time."

"Yeah," said Jack. "I'd like that. Some other time..."

㉛
Dillon's Pants
Tuesday 6 April

Jamie couldn't help staring at the whiteboard in the Hawkstone Academy Team dressing room. As his eyes scanned the diagrams, a flash of recognition lit up Jamie's mind.

The whiteboard was covered with drawings and instructions to teach the Hawkstone players a new skill...

1  **2**

Push the ball diagonally forward ...

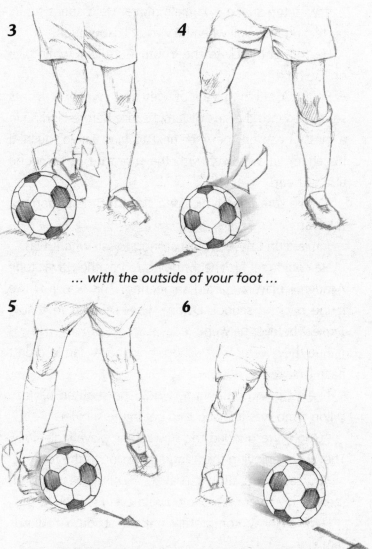

3

4

... with the outside of your foot ...

5

6

... then use the inside of the same foot to tap the ball in the opposite direction and accelerate away...
REMEMBER THE KEY TO THE SNAKE
– DO IT ALL IN ONE MOVEMENT!

It was the *snake* – Jamie's move. He'd spent hours perfecting that skill when he was at Foxborough.

He thought back to the Youth Cup Final when, live on TV, he'd—

Splat. A stinking pair of wet and sweaty Y-fronts squelched into the side of Jamie's face before landing in a messy heap on the floor next to him. Jamie touched his cheek; it was wet with the moisture of someone else's sweat.

"Make sure they're nice and clean for me tomorrow, Johnson!"

Jamie didn't have to turn around to see who it was.

He could feel his cheeks going red as the Hawkstone Academy players started sniggering. This was just like being back at school. Dillon's jibes seemed to follow Jamie wherever he went.

But they weren't at school any more. Jamie didn't have to take this now.

"I ain't doing nothing for you!" he shouted back to Dillon, who was just about to get in the shower.

"Oooh," responded the Hawkstone players gleefully. They were enjoying the rising aggression in the room.

"In case you didn't realize," Dillon responded, menacingly, "your job is to do whatever I tell you to do."

He was now completely naked, striding towards Jamie.

"We're footballers," he said, pointing to his teammates. "And you're not!"

The Hawkstone boys clapped in their appreciation of Dillon's disses.

"That's it, Dillon," they said, goading him on. "Take him down! Give him some proper licks!"

At that moment, Jamie felt more alone than he had ever done in his life.

But he knew one thing: he had to stand up for himself.

"You're right," said Jamie, using all the courage he could muster. "I may not be a footballer... But at least I'm not scum!"

"Oh no, Dillon!" called one of the Hawkstone players. "He's just blatantly disrespected you to your face! What you gonna do about it?"

"I'm gonna do the same thing I've always done: teach the idiot a lesson!"

And with that, Dillon pulled back his fist and sent a pounding punch piling towards Jamie's face.

Instinctively, Jamie snapped his head out of the way, feeling the gust of Dillon's lunge against his cheek.

"Not this time," Jamie said, elbowing the back of Dillon's shoulder blade with such force that he sent Dillon flying to the ground.

For a second, Jamie couldn't believe what had happened.

He looked below him, where Dillon was now lying on the floor, with his face buried in his own dirty underpants!

Jamie wondered where his strength had come from. He'd never been able to lay a hand on Dillon at school. Let alone floor him!

Not that Dillon was down for long. Like an angry bear, he drew himself up to his full, frightening height. Jamie took a pace back. He was in trouble.

There was madness in Dillon's eyes as he marched towards Jamie, who had nowhere else to go. His back was right up against the wall. Jamie took a deep breath and tensed his stomach muscles to prepare them for the onslaught that was about to come…

"OK, time for us to get on with washing this kit, Jamie," said Archie Fairclough, who'd come from nowhere and purposefully placed his body in between Jamie and Dillon. "I've only got a few minutes, then I've got a meeting with Harry Armstrong."

Although Archie was talking to Jamie, he was looking Dillon square in the eye. For a moment, all three of them stood motionless. Then Dillon grimaced and took a step back.

"Yeah, you'd best get him away, Cloughie," he snarled. "We wouldn't want anything nasty to happen to your little assistant…"

"Don't worry," Archie responded while the two boys still glared at each other. "He's learned his lesson. And if he hasn't, I'll teach it to him again. Now go and pick up those pants, Jamie, and we can get on with our job."

If it had been anyone else, Jamie would have told them where to go. No one else could have made Jamie pick up Dillon's stinking pants – or anyone else's, for that matter.

But, for Archie – and for the sake of his job – he did it.

Slowly, he approached the dank, soggy underpants that lay on the moist floor by the showers. With Dillon's evil cackles pricking like thorns into his ears, Jamie lifted the pants up with the very tips of his fingers and quickly flung them into the kit bag with the rest of the dirty gear.

Jamie smelled his fingers. They stank.

"One more incident like that and you're out. Gone," threatened Archie at the end of the day. He hadn't said a word to Jamie since they'd left the Academy Team dressing room. He was furious.

"You are my responsibility," he continued. "And I'm not going to have you and your pride ruining my reputation at this club. You got that?"

"But..." Jamie was desperate to tell Archie everything. That he knew Dillon from school and the things Dillon had done to him down the years. That neither Dillon nor any of those other Hawkstone Academy Team players were good enough to lace Jamie's boots when he'd been a player...

"No buts," countered Archie. "You knew what the job was when you took it. If you don't like it, you can leave. I mean it. But believe me, you'll have no idea what you're throwing away."

Jamie thought for a minute. He remembered what his life had been like before this job.

"Sorry," he said, softly. "It won't happen again."

He felt ashamed of himself now.

"Too right it won't," said Archie. "And you'll thank me for this one day."

Then he tossed Jamie a pair of flashy boots to polish.

On the heels of the boots, written very clearly in indelible marker-pen, were the initials DS.

One Man Down

Friday 23 April

It was a Friday and, as Jamie watched the Hawkstone players train ahead of their big weekend game, his mind drifted towards Mike. He had loved the Hawks his entire life; he would have been so proud that Jamie was now working at the club.

"You know," said Archie, who was standing alongside Jamie, gulping down yet another mug of tea, "I won't be doing this job for ever. If you play your cards right, one day you could take over from me..."

Jamie smiled and was just about to respond when Harry Armstrong suddenly blew his whistle on the training pitch and bellowed: "Hey, Cloughie!"

"Yes, boss! What can I do for you?" asked Archie.

"Your assistant – I need him in goal for the last five minutes; we're one man down."

It wasn't until he felt Archie's eyes resting on him that Jamie realized Harry Armstrong had been talking about him. *He* was the assistant that they wanted to go in goal…

Jamie felt panic surge through him. He didn't know what to do. He was being asked to play football again. And that was unleashing a whole tide of emotions in him.

Jamie started to breathe in and out rapidly. He turned to look at Archie for guidance.

"Well, go on, then!" encouraged Archie. "It's only five minutes!"

Jamie had no option. Only a complete loser would turn down an opportunity like this.

Hesitantly, he jumped over the railings that surrounded the training pitch. Then, with his head down, he half jogged, half walked to the empty goals.

"Come on! Get a move on!" the Hawkstone players were shouting at him.

They couldn't see that Jamie's whole body was shaking with nerves.

"Here you are, son," said Bob Hurst, the Hawkstone goalkeeping coach, throwing Jamie a pair of gloves. "You'll need these."

Alive Again

Jamie stood in the middle of the goal and clapped his gloved hands together. He jumped up and touched the underside of the crossbar.

He didn't know exactly why he did it – he'd just seen other keepers do it, so he felt as though it was the right thing to do.

He just hoped he wouldn't embarrass himself – or Archie, who was watching from the sidelines like a nervous father.

Jamie rubbed his back. For the first time in weeks, it was starting to hurt. Then he thought about the screws that were holding his leg together. He wondered if they were up to this.

Oh, just shut up and enjoy the game! Jamie shouted to his inner demons. He sounded almost like Mike.

Jamie only knew one thing. As the training match got restarted, he felt something that he hadn't felt for months: alive.

To start with, Jamie didn't have that much to do. He came to collect a couple of crosses and even made quite a professional-looking throw out to the full-back.

He was just starting to think this goalkeeping lark was easy, when he was presented with a much sterner test.

Glenn Richardson, who was playing against Jamie, had struck a sixty-yard through-ball for the striker to chase.

Jamie was already a few yards off his line and he thought that he could get to the ball first, so he came out of his area to clear it. But when the backspin on Richardson's pass kicked in, Jamie realized he was in trouble...

It was too late to run back in goal and he was out of his area now so he couldn't pick the ball up either.

The only option he had left was to try and win the race for the ball. But he was clearly second-favourite.

Jamie put his head down, pumped his arms and sprinted towards the ball.

And then something amazing happened.

For those couple of seconds, Jamie felt no pain whatsoever in his body. Every bone, muscle and sinew responded to the situation and Jamie's speed clicked back into gear as though it had never been away. He shot across the turf with pace and grace.

He was sprinting at such speed that not only did he win the race to the ball, but now, with the ball at his feet, he didn't want to stop! He just kept going!

Jamie powered forward at an unbelievable speed.

If he had looked up at that moment, he would have seen Archie Fairclough punching the air with joy. He was so excited that he'd chucked his mug of tea high into the air. As it dropped, it splashed its contents all over the paint on the touchline.

But Jamie's mind was closed to everything that was going on around him. In fact, he wasn't thinking at all. He was simply doing the one thing he truly knew he could do in this world: run with a football.

As he raced down the pitch, Jamie just seemed to be getting faster and faster. He got all the way to the other touchline and whipped in a beautiful, curling cross to the far post…

It was a sensational centre. But no one was there to meet it. Because they had all stopped playing.

Instead, every single Hawkstone player was simply

standing, staring at Jamie. They were in awe of what they had just seen.

It was as though, for those few seconds, Jamie had been in some kind of trance.

But now he had returned to his senses. He looked back towards the empty goal that he had vacated and suddenly realized that he had sprinted the entire length of the pitch at his very top speed.

He'd had no idea his body could still do that.

But it just had.

"Jamie Johnson! I knew you still had it!" Harry Armstrong suddenly yelled, breaking the silence.

Jamie looked up.

"What? How did you know my—"

"Of course I know who you are," said Harry, laughing. "Archie told me the first day you walked in here. I've just been waiting for him to tell me that you were ready."

Jamie immediately looked across at Archie. The wink he received in return told Jamie everything. Archie had known all along...

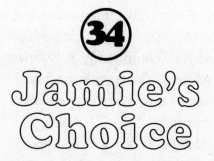

34
Jamie's Choice

"The MRI scans show that all the injuries have entirely healed," said Alistair Ramsey, Hawkstone's chief doctor. "And the agility levels are ... well ... hugely impressive. Are you sure you haven't played any football since the accident, Jamie?"

"I promise I haven't," said Jamie, smiling. He hadn't been able to stop grinning since he'd kicked that football. "The only exercise I've been doing is all the stuff Archie has made me..."

It was only as he said the words that Jamie fully appreciated what had been happening over the last few months. All that lifting, carrying and painting... It had all been part of Archie's plan. Slowly but surely, he'd been nurturing Jamie's recovery. Restoring him back to full fitness.

"Well, I can only tell you that your core stability is as good as, if not better than, eighty per cent of the players in our First Team squad," stated Dr Ramsey.

Jamie and Harry Armstrong sat, listening intently to the doc's analysis. The minute training had finished, Harry had asked Jamie to come to the medical centre to get a full diagnosis.

But now Dr Ramsey had stopped talking.

"And?" asked Armstrong. "Does that mean he's OK to play?"

"I'm afraid it's not quite as simple as that, Harry."

"What do you mean 'it's not that simple'? Either he's fit to play or he's not."

"Let me try and explain," said Dr Ramsey. "Physically, medically even, Jamie is a hundred per cent fit. But where traumas like this have occurred you never truly know the strength of the joint or bone until they are tested … taken to the limit, if you like.

"It may be that Jamie is completely fine, good as new. But it may also be that there is a weakness there and, if he were to sustain a trauma to either his back or leg again, this time, the injuries could be … well, I'm afraid there's no other way to say it … irreversible."

Dr Ramsey seemed to linger for an impossibly long time over the word *irreversible*. Then he looked up and concluded: "Basically, we'll only know when his body is put to the ultimate test."

"By which time it could be too late?" asked Harry Armstrong.

But it wasn't really a question.

As Dr Ramsey left the room, Harry Armstrong looked at Jamie.

"I'm going to be completely honest with you, Jamie," he said. "As a football manager, I'm desperate to have you in my team. I watched you in that Youth Cup Final and I've never seen anything like it. In football terms, it's a no-brainer. You go straight into my First Team squad. That's how good I believe you are. And … God knows we need you...

"But this is not a simple decision, Jamie. We both heard what the doc said – there are serious risks in you playing football again. The question is: are you prepared to take those risks?"

No Regrets

"Please tell me you're joking," said Jeremy, striding around the room like a madman. Jamie had told his mum and Jeremy everything that had happened and that Hawkstone were prepared to put him on a temporary playing contract. He and Jeremy had been arguing for the last half an hour.

"Am I the only one who can see what's happening here?" Jeremy continued. "So he starts playing again and then he gets rejected – or worse still, injured – and what's he left with then? Nothing. Zilch. *Again*… No qualifications, no future, nothing. I say he starts back at school in September and—"

"Oh, for God's sake, Jeremy – it's his dream!" Jamie's mum suddenly declared. "Sometimes you *have* to take a risk to get what you want."

Then she went into the kitchen. Discussion over.

Jamie's mouth hung wide open. So did Jeremy's. Neither of them had ever seen her be so decisive.

For a while, Jamie couldn't work it out. His mum never seemed to take his side any more and now she'd just supported him in the biggest gamble of his life. And then a memory from when he was really young elbowed its way into Jamie's mind, and it explained a lot.

One day, when he'd just started going to school, Jamie had come home one afternoon and asked his mum what the word *motto* meant.

"It's a saying," she'd explained. "An idea that you try to live your life by. Like: *you don't regret what you do do, only what you don't.* That's my motto," she'd smiled. "I think it's a good one."

The next day, Jamie was in the office of the Hawkstone Club Secretary, Eugene Elliott. In front of him was a short-term playing contract.

"Where do I sign, Mr Elliott?" asked Jamie.

"Don't you want to negotiate first?" Eugene Elliott laughed. "Have you got an agent?"

"I don't have an agent any more," Jamie responded. He'd been down that path once before already. "It's not about the money for me."

"Wow," said Eugene Elliott, handing Jamie a pen. "You really are a different breed!"

"I just want to play football," Jamie said. "For Hawkstone."

Then he signed the contract.

The Boy Can Play

Monday 26 April

Jamie laced up his boots and walked out on to the Hawkstone United training pitch.

As a player.

Archie was there, sitting on his mower on the adjacent pitch. He'd said he wasn't going to replace Jamie just yet; in case it didn't work out, Jamie's old job would still be there for him. He gave Jamie a big thumbs up. Jamie returned the gesture.

Jamie hoped that neither Archie nor anyone else would find any specks of sick in the changing room; he'd tried to wipe it all up but there wasn't much time

– he didn't want to be late for his first training session. Jamie had spewed up almost his entire breakfast. He was so nervous, he felt he might just suddenly fall over at any given moment.

It had been almost a year since the Youth Cup Final. That was a lifetime ago.

Almost as soon as they started playing, the ball came to Jamie. But he was so worried about what he was going to do with it when he got it that he didn't control it properly. The ball bounced off his knee and went straight out of play.

The second time that Jamie tried to kick the ball, it went off the wrong side of his boot, gifting possession to the other side. Then, a few minutes later, when Jamie tried to volley in a shot from a glorious Glenn Richardson cross, he thrashed at the ball so wildly that he missed it completely and ended up in a heap on the ground.

Jamie punched the turf and yelled so loudly in frustration that Harry Armstrong actually stopped the game.

The other Hawkstone players were all just staring at him. They weren't even laughing. They felt embarrassed *for* him.

"This some sort of prank, then, is it, gaffer?" asked Glenn Richardson. "One of them TV wind-up programmes where we're supposed to believe that you've signed the lad from maintenance and then someone tells us it's all been a gag?"

"Good question," said Harry Armstrong, smiling at Jamie as he answered. "Could be. You'll have to wait until the end of training to find out, won't you?"

Jamie got to his feet. He looked down at his left leg. One of the scars went all the way up from his shin to his knee. You could still see where the stitches had been inserted.

What did he think he was doing? Did he honestly believe that he could still play football at this level? After everything his body had been through? What had happened in that other training session had been the final bit of football that his body had been willing to offer. Not the start of a new chapter.

"Keep your head still," Harry Armstrong said quietly to Jamie as he picked up the ball. "Everything in sport comes from keeping your head still."

Then Harry suddenly roared: "Play ON!" and he smacked the ball straight at Jamie...

There was no time for Jamie to think. He instinctively controlled the ball on his thigh. It bounced upwards. He let it rest on his forehead for a second, tilting his neck to keep the ball still. Then he flicked the ball up, off his head and into the air. As it dropped, Jamie smashed an inch-perfect fifty-yard cross-field pass to the right-winger way out on the other side of the pitch.

It was one of the best long passes that Jamie had ever played.

"What were you saying again, Glenn?" Harry Armstrong asked his star midfielder as they both followed Jamie's ball out to the wing.

"Nothing," said Glenn Richardson. "Fair enough, gaffer; the boy can play."

"Oh, he can play all right."

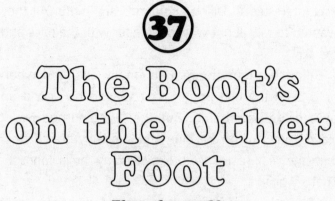

37

The Boot's on the Other Foot

Thursday 13 May

Dillon Simmonds was staring at Archie the kit-man but he wasn't listening to a word he was saying.

All he could think about was Jammy Jamie Johnson.

He couldn't believe that Johnson had suddenly gone from being Archie's little assistant to training with the Hawkstone First Team squad.

Why was it that everyone always thought Johnson was the special one? Winger was an easy position to play, anyway; they didn't have to do any work.

Dillon thought back to when he was at Kingfield School. Before Johnson had joined, Dillon had always been known as the best player, but then this skinny ginger kid arrived from nowhere and suddenly no one was interested in Dillon Simmonds any more. All they wanted to talk about was this winger with the pace and the skill.

Dillon thought things had finally changed when he'd been the first boy in their year to be signed up by a professional club. But then who turned up at Hawkstone out of the blue and suddenly got to train with the First Team? Who else? Jammy Jamie Johnson. That's who.

"OK, lads, I just need half an hour of your time," said Archie Fairclough. "As some of you may know, I've just lost my assistant ... which means I need a bit of help with the kit. And the manager has been kind enough to say that you lucky lot are the ones that can help me!"

A collective groan spread around the academy boys.

"Do we have to? Why us?" they pleaded.

"Oh, stop moaning," snapped Archie. "A bit of manual work won't kill you!"

Then he started chucking different pairs of football boots at the young Hawkstone players.

"The First Team are going to play the biggest match in this club's history on Sunday," said Archie. "So they'll need their boots in shiny, faultless, pristine condition..."

Dillon just about caught the pair of boots that Archie flung at him. He could have sworn that Archie had thrown them harder than he'd needed to.

Dillon dipped his towel into the bucket of warm, soapy water and began picking the mud out from the studs and polishing the leather of the boots. He scrubbed hard at the heel to reveal the initials that had been written there.

The letters slowly appeared like ghosts from Dillon's nightmare... JJ.

Life Goes in Circles

Saturday 15 May – The day before the last Premier League games of the season
The day before
Foxborough v Hawkstone United

Jamie turned off the TV. All the sports stations had wall-to-wall previews of the Foxborough–Hawkstone game.

They were all speculating about the team news. But none of them knew about Jamie. Harry Armstrong hadn't told anyone. He wanted to keep it up his sleeve.

"Something to give Brian Robertson a little shock just before kick-off," he'd told Jamie.

Funny how life goes in circles, Jamie thought to himself as he turned off the light above his bed. Here he was, staying in the same Travelodge that he and his dad had stayed in when they had first come up to Foxborough all those months ago.

He tried to imagine where his dad was now and what he would be doing. Probably trying to rip someone else off. Jamie pictured him – sitting in a pub somewhere tomorrow, watching the game. Then, suddenly, he would see Jamie Johnson come on to the pitch.

Jamie hoped his dad would choke on his beer.

Jamie's eyelids began to droop as his body wriggled into a snug position.

Now, in the darkness, his mind was leaving this room and travelling somewhere else.

His memory was returning to a place it had been before and to a moment that had changed the course of Jamie's life...

Jamie was standing on the side of a road. He recognized the road. But he could not yet place it.

He could hear voices behind him: soft at first, now getting louder and more aggressive.

"Yeah, he's just a little boy!" they were shouting. No, not *they*; only one voice, one nasty, vicious voice. "Go home, little boy," the voice was shouting. "Go back to your mummy."

Back in the hotel, Jamie's body twitched and his eyelids flickered as, beneath them, that night's events continued to unfold for him.

From above, Jamie could see himself standing in the road, turning around to cross back towards the other Foxborough players...

"No!" Jamie wanted to scream to himself, to warn himself, but his mouth was locked shut. He couldn't stop himself doing it...

Jamie wasn't looking as he started to cross the road, but his head turned when he heard the screech of braking tyres.

The car crashed into Jamie's body – a body that had been protected and prized as one of football's most valuable assets – and tossed it on to the bonnet.

Now he could see himself bouncing off the window and over the car; he was about to hit the ground—

And then suddenly Jamie was awake. He was bolt upright with sweat pouring down his forehead. It was a cold sweat, a freezing sweat. Jamie's whole body was shivering and his eyes were wide open with fright.

He looked across to the alarm clock by his bed. It was four a.m. There were exactly twelve hours to go until kick-off.

39

Chance to be a Hero

Sunday 16 May – The last day of the Premier League season

The Lair
Foxborough v Hawkstone United

The bell rang in the Hawkstone dressing room. It was showtime.

"OK, lads," shouted Harry Armstrong, clapping his hands together. "I know I don't have to say much today. It's quite simple. If we lose, this club goes down, more than a few of us will be looking for new clubs and Hawkstone United could well go out of business.

"Whatever you've got in your bodies and in your hearts, I want you to give it all out there today. Everything. I want you to think about all those fans that have come up the motorway to support us. This club means the world to them. Just remember that.

"And, lads, there's good news too; it's that there's no pressure on you at all today. If it doesn't go our way, I'll take all the blame. No problem. But, if there's glory to be had out there, it's all yours.

"And believe me, if we can pull this off, you lot will be heroes at this club for the rest of your lives! Now let's go out there and do this!"

"Come on!" roared the Hawkstone players, leaping to their feet.

Jamie jumped up and clenched his fist as tight as he could.

He was sure that his whole career, his whole life even, had been building towards this day.

The Hawkstone players exited their dressing room and lined up in the tunnel. They were all jogging on the spot, nervously chewing gum and tipping their heads from side to side.

Jamie was kicking a ball against the wall when he felt a sharp prod in his rib. He turned around.

"What's up?" said Bolt, locking Jamie's palm in his own and pulling it to his chest.

"Bolt! How's it going? Good to see you, bruv!"

"Whoa!" said Bolt, suddenly taking a surprised step back, looking at Jamie suspiciously. "What's happened to you?"

"What do you mean?"

"You been on the weights or something?"

Jamie realized what Bolt was talking about: his new physique. It was true, he must have grown about two inches and put on a stone in muscle since their days together in the Foxborough Youth Team.

"Yeah – you could say that," Jamie smiled, remembering how on his first day with Archie he'd hardly been able to lift a five-a-side goal. Within a couple of months he'd been able to march the whole length of the pitch carrying the goal above his head.

"Hopefully I'll see you out there today," said Bolt. "I'm sub. I played for the First Team in the Cup last week."

"That's wicked!" said Jamie. "Told you we'd all make it! What about Xabi, where's he?"

Bolt's face dropped.

"He's gone back home," he said, almost apologizing. "They sold him back to his local club but kept a buy-back clause."

"What happened?" asked Jamie.

"He was getting homesick. Turned out he had a

161

girlfriend back home and he was missing her so much it was starting to affect his game."

The Foxborough players were coming out of their dressing room now.

"OK, man. Good luck and we'll catch up later," said Bolt, slapping Jamie on the back as he went.

"Yeah – see you, mate," said Jamie.

But the smile was wiped off Jamie's face as soon as the Foxborough team lined up in the tunnel.

Standing next to Jamie, wearing a poisonous expression on his face, was Rick Morgan.

Morgan was glaring at Jamie as though he wanted to destroy him.

Jamie took a deep breath and looked straight ahead. Somehow, he'd completely forgotten that his direct opponent today would be the man whose taunts, almost exactly a year ago, had nearly wrecked Jamie's entire career.

Today, they would sort this out once and for all.

On the pitch.

Battle Begins

"And you join us here in Foxborough for a terrific climax to the Premier League season. What a game we have in store for you today.

"The hosts, Foxborough, need only a point to win the League title for the third year in a row, while Hawkstone United come here knowing that only a win will be good enough to save them from relegation.

"And even the team line-ups are not without a little drama.

"Now, who remembers Jamie Johnson? He was the young winger who put in a starring performance for Foxborough in last season's Youth Cup Final, only to be cruelly struck down in a shocking car accident only days later.

"That was end of the young prodigy's career. Or so we thought. Today Jamie Johnson is back ... but there has been a change: Johnson is now playing for Hawkstone United!

"Johnson has only just started playing again, but player-manager Harry Armstrong clearly believes he has nothing to lose today, so he's put Johnson in from the start!

"Buckle up, people. This could be a classic... It's Foxborough versus Hawkstone ... and it's live!"

Jamie put his hand to his forehead to shield his eyes from the sun. He waved to his mum, Jeremy and Jack. They were in with the rest of the Hawks fans. He was so glad they had made the journey. He had a good feeling about today.

As the referee put the whistle to his mouth, Harry Armstrong turned around to look at his troops one last time.

Now was the moment for any final instructions. Any last words of inspiration. But Harry didn't say a word. It had all been said.

They knew what they had to do.

The Lair
Kick-Off
Foxborough 0 - 0 Hawkstone United

As the whistle went to get the game under way, the noise from both sets of fans made it seem like there were a million people crammed into The Lair. The stadium was practically vibrating!

And the players responded to the atmosphere. This was more like a battle between warring gladiators than a game of football.

One particular confrontation on the halfway line between the two hard men, Dave Lewington and Harry Armstrong, was so colossal that they almost burst the ball as they went in for the tackle!

Even the referee was playing his part. Apart from one early booking – Rick Morgan for a deliberate handball – he seemed prepared to allow most things to go.

The intensity was unbelievable. Neither team were prepared to give any ground. How could they? There was too much at stake.

There was nothing between the two sides until, on eighteen minutes, Glenn Richardson decided it was time to interrupt the warfare with a moment of artistry. He produced one of the finest pieces of skill ever witnessed in the Premier League...

He collected the ball from a throw-in, controlling it on his thigh with his back to goal. Then, as the ball dropped, he turned and struck a full-blooded volley high into the air. At first, no one in the ground was quite sure what he was attempting; they simply saw the ball fly up into the afternoon sky.

But as the ball arced and began its descent, and the Foxborough keeper suddenly turned and scampered back towards his goal, people began to see what Glenn Richardson's football vision had shown him a few seconds before: that he could take on a shot from the halfway line!

Time stood still as the Foxborough keeper desperately raced back to try and tip the ball over. He just managed to get a hand to it. But it wasn't enough. He could only palm the ball further into the goal.

It was in! Hawkstone had scored! They were on course!

The Lair
Foxborough 0 - 1 Hawkstone United
6 Richardson, 19

Every single Hawkstone player mobbed Glenn Richardson. Jamie was so excited he even kissed Glenn's boot!

"What a goal!" screamed Jamie. "You the man!"

Now the Hawks were flying. Their confidence was soaring. And on their next attack, it was time for Jamie to get in on the act.

As the ball came to him, his feet felt springy and powerful. He was completely in control of his body. This was his destiny. The time had come.

He took on Rick Morgan for pace and shot past him like a brand-new Ferrari overtaking a clapped-out old banger. Morgan only just managed to get back in time to block the cross and concede a corner.

Jamie bounced over to take the set piece. He had energy and confidence coursing through his veins. He had football power in his core. He was back and he knew it.

He raised his hands in the air to clap the Hawks fans behind the goal. They were all shouting his name.

And there above them, in one of the posh executive boxes, smiling down eerily, was a face that Jamie thought he would never see again.

It was his dad.

(41)
One Way Out

"Go on, Jamie! Use your skills! Whip it in!" shouted the Hawks fans, as Jamie prepared to take the corner. "Put it in the mixer!"

But Jamie felt sick. He felt weak. His legs were about to give way. He couldn't believe that, after all this time, his dad would just show up. Today of all days. Hadn't he done enough damage?

Jamie stepped towards the ball. He tried to curl it into the middle but his boot struck the corner flag and he fell flat on his face. It must have been the worst corner in the history of football.

"*Oh dear, that's not what Jamie Johnson would have intended,*" said the TV commentator, up in the gantry. "*After such a positive start, perhaps nerves are beginning to get the better of the young man."*

The rest of the first half, Jamie was a pale imitation of a footballer. A pale imitation of himself.

He just couldn't focus on the game. When his teammates had the ball and looked up for someone to pass to, Jamie didn't call for it. He wasn't making any runs either.

His sharpness… His hunger… It was gone.

All he seemed to be able to think about was his dad. He hated the fact that he was here, looking down at Jamie.

Where had he been when Jamie needed him?

The Lair
Half-Time
Foxborough 0 - 1 Hawkstone United
6 Richardson, 19

As the half-time whistle blew, Jamie sprinted off the pitch before anyone else. He could hear the Hawks fans barracking him as he went.

"Get him off, Harry!"

"He's too young, Armstrong, make the change!"

"We have to defend our lead, Harry – we can't afford to play a kid now!"

And Jamie couldn't blame them. He would have shouted the same.

He sensed there was only one way out of this situation.

"What the hell's going on?!" Harry Armstrong roared at Jamie as soon as they got into the dressing room. "You start like a house on fire and then, for the last ten minutes, you can hardly kick the ball? It's like you don't even want to be out there. What's the problem?!"

"I'll explain later, boss," said Jamie, standing up and walking towards the dressing-room door. "But right now I've got to go and do something."

"What are you talking about?!" raged Harry. "You can sit down like the rest of the lads and listen to what I've got to say."

"Seriously, boss. I can't. This is just something I have to do."

"If you walk out that door, Jamie, I'm subbing you. That's it."

"I promise, boss, I'll explain everything. Just give me five minutes."

Jamie didn't wait to hear the response. He left the Hawkstone dressing room.

Once he'd explained to the policeman where he wanted to go to, it was only a matter of seconds before Jamie found himself in the Foxborough boardroom, which fell into a confused silence as the young winger, still dressed in his Hawkstone strip, entered the room.

Everyone turned to look at Jamie, but he was staring at just one person.

"Jamie!" said his dad, putting down his glass of wine and walking over to greet his son. Jamie could now see the falseness of the smile that had fooled him for so long.

"What are *you* doing here?" demanded Jamie. He made no attempt to keep his voice down.

"What do you mean, what am I doing here?" smiled his dad, trying to usher Jamie into a corner so he wouldn't cause a scene in front of everyone else in the boardroom.

"I'm here for you, Jamie, like always. Oh, and by the way, I've had a word with the Foxborough chairman and they're very interested in—"

"Where have you been for the last year, then?" snarled Jamie. He hadn't moved. He was standing right in the centre of the room.

"When you thought I wasn't worth anything to you, you just dropped me. Like I was a piece of rubbish. Well, I'm not rubbish! And I'm not stupid, either."

"Of course you're not, Jamie. Look, I'm sorry, I just had other business stuff," said Jamie's dad, trying to put his arm around Jamie's shoulder.

"Don't touch me!" shouted Jamie. Now the whole room had turned to stare at them.

"As far as I'm concerned, you're not my dad, and I never want to speak to you again. You're nothing to me."

As he said the words, Jamie felt a burden lift from his chest. He felt relieved.

"Fine," said Ian Reacher, and suddenly the smoothness in his voice was replaced by dark venom. His true colours were coming through. "But remember, Jamie, you wouldn't be anything without me. I'm the one who got you here."

"Wrong," said Jamie. "You're the one that left me."

As Jamie walked out of the boardroom, he saw the Foxborough chairman speak to two of the security guards. The guards approached Ian Reacher and asked him to leave.

"All right!" Reacher snapped. "I'm going! Get your hands off me!"

Jamie ran back to the changing room as fast as he could, but the players were already out on the pitch.

As Jamie sprinted down the tunnel, his heart sank. He was too late. He could see the fourth official was holding up the board. There was going to be a substitution.

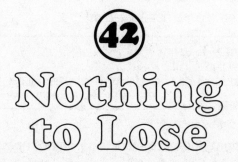

42
Nothing to Lose

"Welcome back to The Lair, where we can bring you news of a big half-time substitution. This should shake things up a bit... But it's not the change we were expecting ... Jamie Johnson is still on for Hawkstone...

"In fact, it's Foxborough who have made the change. They have brought on their prolific young centre forward Antony Asamoah..."

"You better have a good excuse, Jamie," said Harry Armstrong as Jamie dashed out on to the pitch to join the rest of the Hawkstone team.

"I'll explain everything to you later, gaffer," Jamie insisted. "I promise you."

"Forget about that," said Armstrong. "Just do your talking on the pitch."

Then the second half kicked off.

The Lair
Second Half
Foxborough 0 - 1 Hawkstone United
6 Richardson. 19

Bolt's height and pace made an instant impact on the game. The Hawkstone defence had to drop far deeper because they were scared of him running in behind.

But what was even worse was that Jamie could tell instantly that Bolt was on fire. He was on a mission.

As Hawkstone were preparing to defend a free-kick on the edge of their area, Jamie ran back into his own half and shouted to his teammates: "Oi! Watch him, yeah?" pointing to his old room-mate. "He's dangerous."

Almost as soon as Jamie had uttered those words, Dave Lewington stepped up and floated in a beautiful free-kick to the far post. It bounced once before Bolt, as brave a lion, dived in where boots were flying to get in a header. It was a bullet of an effort. And it was Foxborough's equalizer.

"No!" Jamie yelled, kicking out at the advertising board by the side of the pitch. He'd *warned* them about Bolt!

From that moment, the Foxborough fans couldn't stop singing.

"Champions! Champions! Champions!" they cried, roaring with pride.

They knew a draw was good enough for them to retain the league and they were confident they would get it.

And while the Foxborough fans were cheering and lifting up replica trophies in the stands, on the pitch, their players simply kept the ball. It was all they needed to do.

Every time the ball went out of play for a goal kick, the Foxborough keeper took what seemed like an age to retrieve it, carefully place it down, take a deep run back and then launch it into the air. Everyone could see he was running down the clock, but there was nothing the Hawkstone players could do about it.

It was during one of these breaks in play that Harry Armstrong sprinted up to Jamie.

"Jamie, I want to make a change," he said to his young winger.

"No, boss, please don't sub me! I can still do something, I can feel it!" Jamie pleaded.

"No, that's not what I mean," said Harry, lowering his voice so the Foxborough players couldn't hear what he was saying. "I want you to come in off the wing, play in the hole behind the strikers. And just stay up there, don't worry about coming back."

"Sure," smiled Jamie. He liked playing in that position. "But who's going to do my defending?"

"You're looking at him," said Harry. "I just want you to stay central and get yourself involved in this game. We need you on the ball."

"OK, boss ... if you're sure?"

"Eh, Jamie," said Harry, throwing his hands up in the air as he jogged back into position. "What've we got to lose?!"

43

Moment of Truth

Jamie looked up at the massive clock behind the Foxborough goal. There were now only six minutes left. Six minutes to save Hawkstone United.

Jamie knew, everyone knew, that if they went down, Hawkstone would go bust. They had too many debts to survive outside of the Premier League. It was simple: relegation would kill Hawkstone.

Jamie couldn't let that happen. Not to the Hawks. They were his club. Always would be.

He had to do something.

"Yes," Jamie yelled as soon as he found a yard of space. Harry Armstrong laid the ball into his feet. "Turn!"

he shouted, to tell Jamie there was no one behind him.

Jamie spun and accelerated towards the Foxborough goal. He weaved past two challenges, pushing the ball on to his favoured left foot. Now Rick Morgan surged across to try and stop him.

One of Jamie's step-overs was enough to take him past Morgan. He was close now, close to the Foxborough goal. The ground had fallen silent; everyone was waiting to see what Jamie Johnson would do next.

The clock seemed to stop as Jamie looked up. He saw that the keeper was off his line. He was going to try the chip … but he was taking too long … Morgan had caught him up now … Morgan was lunging at him now…

Before Jamie could get his shot away, Morgan had flown into him from behind, ferociously mowing him down.

He trapped both of Jamie's legs under his heavy frame in the challenge.

Jamie crumpled to the ground.

He could see Rick Morgan spitting as he stood up and looked at Jamie, bearing his fangs.

For a second, Jamie thought he was going to be OK.

And then the pain came.

Jamie's body gasped for air. He felt as though he was drowning in a sea of agony. He held his hand out in the air. He needed the medics. He felt his left leg. It was trembling… But was it broken?

On the Hawkstone bench, Archie Fairclough put his head in his hands. This was his worst fear.

In the stands, Jamie's mum clutched Jeremy's hand. She was pinching it so tightly her knuckles were going blue.

Next to her, Jack Marshall closed her eyes. Her body shivered as she breathed in desperately. Jamie's pain was hurting her too.

"You OK, son?" said the referee, leaning over Jamie's prone body on the ground. "Do you need a stretcher?"

Jamie couldn't talk. The pain had paralysed him. He could only cover his eyes with his hand to hide the hurt.

Jamie had never felt torture like this before. It ripped up through his leg like a hundred daggers all stabbing him at the same time.

He wanted to cry, die, or whatever it took to make the pain go away.

He saw his teammates' anguished faces huddle above him as he fell deeper and deeper into the ground. They were talking to him but he couldn't hear them.

Somewhere in the back of his brain, a word was ricocheting around Jamie's senses: *irreversible* ... *irreversible* ... *irreversible*...

"Where is it, Jamie?" asked the Hawkstone physio, rushing to get his painkilling spray out of his bag. "Tell me where it hurts."

But Jamie couldn't speak.

The Test

Almost as if to protect himself from the pain he was in, Jamie's mind had left the stadium and gone to a different place...

He was a little kid again, back at Mike's house, sitting on the couch, showing Mike all the grazes and cuts on his knees from where the other boys had fouled him.

They'd always fouled him. It was the only way they could stop him.

Mike was putting a plaster over his wounds and scuffing up Jamie's hair with the palm of his hand...

Back on the pitch, the referee was calling Rick Morgan over to him.

"You've had your last chance," he told Morgan. "You knew what you were doing."

He was reaching for his pocket now…

And then, suddenly, a massive roar erupted from the Hawkstone end of the ground. The Hawkstone fans had leapt to their feet. They were cheering now, punching the air.

Because they had seen Jamie Johnson slowly haul himself to his feet!

As he stood up, the first thing that Jamie saw was the referee reaching for his red card to send Rick Morgan off.

"No! Don't do that!" appealed Jamie, limping towards the referee.

"What? Are you OK?" said the startled ref, looking Jamie up and down.

"Yeah, no problem," smiled Jamie.

Inside he was still in agony, but he didn't want anyone to know. Least of all Rick Morgan.

"Look, I'm sure Rick didn't mean it, ref," said Jamie. "I'm fine. Let him stay on. Let's play eleven versus eleven."

It was difficult to see who was more confused, Rick Morgan or the referee. They both looked at Jamie as though he'd just come back from the dead. And neither of them could work out why he was trying to save his direct opponent from being sent off…

In the end, the referee simply shook his head and

said, "All right, Rick. But this is your last chance!"

Then he put his card away.

"How's the leg?" Harry Armstrong shouted across to Jamie.

The Hawkstone player-manager looked nervous. If anything happened to Jamie, he'd never forgive himself.

Even though his leg was still throbbing and sore, Jamie smiled back at his manager.

He was smiling because as the pain started to ease with each passing second, Jamie knew that something huge had just happened.

Little did he know it, but Rick Morgan had just done Jamie the biggest favour of his life: he'd given Jamie the tackle that he'd needed to prove, once and for all, that he was over his injury.

"I'm gonna be fine, Harry," Jamie yelled. "My leg … it just passed the test!"

45
Slaying the Wolf

Jamie bent down and straightened his shin pad. Then he looked up and stared Rick Morgan straight in the eye.

You're only on the pitch because I saved you from being sent off, Jamie said with his glare. *You're on this pitch because I want you on this pitch…*

And now I am going to finish you.

"Play it short," Jamie whispered to Glenn Richardson, who was standing over the free-kick.

Without saying anything, while the Foxborough wall was still trying to organize itself, Richardson flicked the ball subtly to his left. To Jamie…

Jamie collected the ball and charged towards Rick Morgan. He charged at him with such speed and power that Morgan seemed spellbound, unable to react.

"Come on," Jamie roared aloud as he soared towards Morgan. "Let's see how hard you are now, *Wolf*!"

Every single Hawkstone fan rose to his or her feet. Jamie Johnson was in full flight.

Jamie passed the ball from one foot to the other as he approached Morgan. Then he lifted his head and looked up at his opponent.

In his eyes, he could see Morgan's fear. They both knew that Jamie was going to take him. It was just a case of when. And how…

Now! Jamie shouted to himself inside his brain. *Take him now! Destroy him!*

And with that, Jamie dug deep into his body to find another level; a level he'd never been to before. From somewhere deep inside, he found an extra yard of pace.

As he rocketed forward with a lightning burst of speed, he felt so powerful it was almost as if he were running with the strength of two people.

He swept the ball outside and inside the full-back, hypnotizing Morgan with his snake skill.

Morgan's ageing body could not keep up with the

rapid changes in direction. His legs twisted around themselves as they tried to chase after Jamie. But it was useless; Jamie was too quick...

So, in the end, after all his taunts and threats, the only thing Rick Morgan could do as Jamie sped away from him was ... fall over.

He sat on his bum like a baby.

Jamie didn't bother to look around. He was clear.

He cut into the area and drew back his left leg.

It was the leg that had been in plaster. The leg that had lost half its muscle mass while Jamie had been in hospital. The leg that was held together by a bunch of metal screws.

Jamie gathered all the power his body had ever possessed and channelled it into a strike. His foot flashed into the ball, pelting a supersonic rocket of a shot soaring towards the goal.

It was unstoppable.

The ball scorched into the top right-hand corner of the goal. It nearly ripped a hole right through the net!

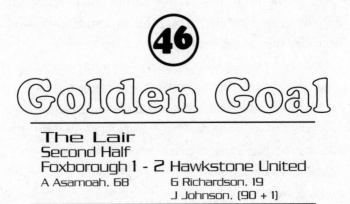

46

Golden Goal

The Lair
Second Half
Foxborough 1 - 2 Hawkstone United
A Asamoah, 68   G Richardson, 19
                       J Johnson, (90 + 1)

As the ball went in, Jamie remained perfectly still. For a single second, he looked up towards the sky and smiled.

He knew who he'd scored that goal for…

Then he turned to stare at the Foxborough bench. Foxborough, the club who'd released him. The club who'd told him his career was over.

He wanted to run over to them, point to the name on the back of his shirt and shout: "Jamie Johnson! That's who I am! I told you I'd come back!"

But before he could do any of that, or even kiss the Hawkstone badge on his shirt, he was pulverized by his teammates. They collapsed into a human pile of joy. They were shrieking in delight and relief. Their wild screams sounded like a group of apes in the jungle!

While they were celebrating on the ground, Archie Fairclough sprinted out of the Foxborough dugout and dive-bombed on top of them! Then he ran over to the Hawks fans and ripped off his shirt to reveal a T-shirt underneath, which said:

We are staying up!
We are staying up!

The Hawkstone fans were now roaring his message back to him as he did a little jig of celebration in front of them. Archie knew the referee would probably send him to the stands for this but he didn't care. There were only a couple of seconds left. Hawkstone were going to do it. They were going to stay up. And his old maintenance assistant was the one who'd scored the goal!

Meanwhile, in the Foxborough dugout, Brian Robertson folded his arms aggressively across his chest. He knew the game was up. He'd just seen the Premier League title stolen away from them by the boy they'd released.

"The kid's a flipping star!" he shouted angrily. "We should never have let him go."

Sitting next to him, Tommy Taylor nodded back enthusiastically.

"You're right, boss. We should never have let him go, boss."

"For God's sake!" Robertson roared. "I just said that!"

"It wasn't simply a good goal," the TV commentator said, as millions of people at home watched the referee blow his final whistle. *"It was a goal that saved an entire football club. Now that truly is a* golden goal*!"*

The Lair
Full-Time
Foxborough 1 - 2 Hawkstone United

A Asamoah, 68	G Richardson, 19
	J Johnson, (90 + 1)

Hawkstone United stay in the Premier League

Extra-Time

"Can we have a quick interview, Jamie?" asked Esther Vaughan, as the Hawkstone players celebrated in front of their fans. It was the sweetest victory any of them had ever experienced.

Jamie smiled at Esther. Then he walked straight past her.

"We're live on TV, Jamie," she shouted desperately. Her director was in her ear, demanding she get Johnson. Johnson was the only one the people at home were interested in.

"It'll be good for your profile, Jamie! Where are you going?"

The reporter turned and motioned for the cameras to follow Jamie. He'd run behind the Hawkstone goal and had now made his way into the crowd.

The fans were lifting him up above their heads, carrying him on an ocean of pride, up towards the top of the stand.

The reporter may not have known where Jamie was

going, but he did. He was going to see the people that mattered most…

The first thing he did was hug his mum.

"Jamie!" she said. "What an unbelievable goal you scored! Right in the top corner!"

Jamie smiled. It sounded as though his mum was actually getting into her football! And she wasn't the only one. Jamie suddenly saw that Jeremy had ripped off his shirt and was swinging it around his head, dancing like a madman with the other Hawks fans around him! He'd even tied a Hawkstone scarf around his forehead like a bandanna!

Jamie turned to look at Jack… He moved towards her. She smiled and clasped her hands around his neck. Then she whispered something into his ear.

"JJ … what took you so long?"

Jamie just looked at her. Then they both started laughing.

"Well played, Jamie," said Dave Lewington, shaking Jamie's hand as Jamie got back down to the pitch. Dave was the only Foxborough player, besides Bolt, who'd been man enough to congratulate the Hawkstone team.

Jamie looked at the other Foxborough players. They were all in a state of shock. None of them had actually believed it was possible that little Hawkstone United could come to the mighty Foxborough and stop them winning the league.

As he watched Rick Morgan slink his way back down the tunnel, Jamie smiled. He'd just remembered something he'd learned at school. Wolves can only survive in packs.

"Jamie!" begged Esther Vaughan as the Hawkstone players headed past her and into the tunnel. "Please, just give us a couple of minutes. Your fans want to hear from you."

Jamie thought for a second.

"Sure," he said. "No problem."

"Thanks, Gary," said Esther breathlessly to the presenter into her microphone.

"Yes, I'm delighted to say that we can now speak to the star of today's show, Jamie Johnson... And Jamie, the first thing to ask is: who writes your scripts? You couldn't have scored at a better time, could you?"

"Yeah, it was a great time to get a goal," agreed Jamie, squirting water over his head to cool himself down. "Obviously, credit to the gaffer for playing me. He took a big risk and I'm glad it paid off for him. The lads are all buzzing!"

"I bet they are!" beamed Esther. "Not many teams come here and beat Foxborough on their own patch.

You must be looking forward to the future after that. Do you think this team can challenge for the League next season?"

"We've got a good bunch of players here, but I think we're just going to enjoy today at the moment," said Jamie, raising his hand up to acknowledge the jubilant Hawks fans who were all singing his name. "This club means a lot to a lot of people. And I'm one of them."

Jamie looked at Esther as she was about to ask her next question. There was no doubt about it – she was more nervous than he was.

"Great... And what about that tackle, just before you scored? You looked in real pain. What was going through your mind at that moment?"

Jamie smiled and looked straight into the camera.

"I was thinking about a piece of advice someone gave me a long time ago," he said. "That if people foul you, it means they're scared of you. You've just got to keep coming back for more."

Interview with Dan Freedman

You've been to the World Cup twice, what was it like?

Before becoming an author, I worked as a journalist with the England Football Team. That meant living in the team hotel, having breakfast with players like Wayne Rooney and Steven Gerrard and then going to watch them train and play in the World Cup Finals. They were some of the greatest experiences of my life. I realize how lucky I was and I thought about those times a lot when I was writing this book.

Can you do all of Jamie's best moves?

Of course I can – I'm a phenomenal footballer, one of the best in the world. See, that's the good thing about being an author: you can just make stuff up.

Who are your favourite footballers at the moment?

You can't ignore Messi's majestic talent and I absolutely love the way that Xavi never ever loses the ball. Gerrard for his passion and loyalty to his club and, for the future, Jack Wilshere. So young but soooo good!

You visit lots of schools – what's the funniest question you've been asked?

Lots of kids seem fascinated to know what car I drive (a Golf, if you must know). Some ask me if I ever get bored of football (no). And one boy asked me which footballer had the biggest appetite when it came to meal times! The school visits are great fun because they are a chance for me to meet the people that I write the books for.

Who is the most famous person you've interviewed?

Take your pick: David Beckham, Cristiano Ronaldo, Sir Alex Ferguson. At the time, I had to pretend that it was no big deal and that I was all cool about it but inside I was thinking: "Oh my God! I can't believe I'm interviewing him!"

So have you ever had a kick around with Wayne Rooney?

No – I think I would be too worried about injuring him if I timed a tackle wrong! That would be a disaster! I did once get to play against Demetrio Albertini though. He was one of the best midfielders in the world when I was growing up – he won the Champions League with AC Milan. I played against him in midfield in a friendly game. Would you believe me if I told you we won?!

What inspires you to write these books?

When I was younger I wasn't a massive reader. People used to tell me to read all the time but there were no books out there that excited me. They all seemed boring. The Jamie Johnson series is for people out there who are like I was. I try to write the kind of books that I would have been desperate to read.

What's the best game you've ever been to?

In 2002, I was in Japan for the World Cup quarter-final: Brazil v England. It doesn't get much bigger than that!

Jamie Johnson books are often about triumphing over the odds. Can you give us any tips on how to become a professional footballer?

I think it's about your physical and mental dedication. Are you training as hard as you can? Are you working on your weaker foot? Do you believe in yourself? Are you trying to improve every time you play? And, if you get knocked back, how will you react? If you come back stronger, you've got half a chance.

And the other thing to remember is that even if you don't make it as a professional footballer, there are so many other jobs that you can get which involve football. Doctor, physiotherapist, coach, architect... The possibilities are all there, it's a case of going for your goals.